DARK HARBOR

DAVID K. WILSON

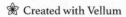 Created with Vellum

1

SAM LAWSON SLOWLY PULLED HIMSELF BACK TO CONSCIOUSNESS, wincing at the burning pain shooting in the back of his head. He was lying on his side on a hardwood floor, but he wasn't sure where. Everything was blurry and spinning, and all he could hear was a deafening ringing in his ears.

"Hello?" he called out, trying to get his bearings.

There was no answer.

He touched the source of pain on the back of his head and was relieved that he felt no blood. Only a massive goose egg where someone must have hit him.

He squinted and strained to focus his vision, but it was hard to find a focal point.

Where am I?

He attempted to recall the events leading up to his attack, but the memories were lost in the fog. He knew he needed to get up, so he rolled onto his stomach and tried to push himself up off the floor. But he was too weak and he collapsed back to the ground with a thud.

He laid there, his head to the side. The cold floor pressed against his cheek. He began to feel the veil slowly lifting. The blurriness was going away. The spinning was slowing down. The ringing was subsiding. He could make out the muffled sounds of a wind chime outside. He remembered those wind chimes. But from where?

He became aware of the unmistakable scent of gunpowder. Out of reflex, he immediately reached for the Glock 22 in his shoulder holster.

But it was missing.

He let out a loud groan as he pulled himself up on his elbows and looked around in the blackness, trying to adjust his eyes to the dark.

What was that on the other side of the room?

He squinted harder. There was definitely something there.

Or someone.

Had he been with someone else? He struggled to pull the buried memories back into his consciousness as he stared at what he was now certain was a person.

"You okay?" he asked.

But the shadowy mass didn't respond.

Remembering he had a cell phone, Sam pulled it from the back pocket of his jeans. His hand-to-eye coordination was still scrambled as he struggled to open the screen. Finally, the phone sprang to life and the light from the screen cast a faint blue glow over the room.

Sam turned the screen toward the person lying across from him but still couldn't make out the face. What he could see was blood.

Lots of blood.

2

3 DAYS EARLIER...

Sam smiled at the feeling of the cold ocean spraying on his face.

It was a gorgeous early May afternoon as the large ferry sped across Vineyard Sound toward its destination in Oak Bluffs. Sam had positioned himself on the upper deck of the ship so he could enjoy the hour-long ride across the Atlantic. As the ferry cut through the choppy waters, wind whipped through Sam's brown hair. Even though it was probably in the upper-70s, the wind made it feel much colder.

The ferry hit another wave, creating more spray. Sam let out a small laugh. He felt like a little kid on vacation. It wasn't like he had never seen the ocean before. He'd been deep sea fishing in Galveston and Corpus Christi and had even been to Cozumel once. But Martha's Vineyard was a different world to him. This was the place where presidents and musicians and movie stars lived.

Sam looked around to see if he could spot anyone famous

on the ferry, but the passengers were clearly not a movie star crowd. Granted, it wasn't quite tourist season yet. He imagined things would change a lot in the next month.

The ferry slowed as it neared Oak Bluffs and Sam took in the island. He watched as the ferry pulled into the harbor and was impressed with the captain's precision as the massive ship aligned gently next to the dock.

A voice bellowed over the speakers to announce their arrival, and Sam flung his duffel bag over his shoulder and joined the other passengers as they headed toward the dock. Butterflies began to flutter in his stomach. Partly in excitement of this impromptu vacation, but mostly in anticipation of surprising Carla Davenport.

Carla and Sam had been dating for less than a year with a few rounds of breaking up and making up. They had recently gone through a bit of a rough patch, but seemed to be getting back on track. Unfortunately, right when things were taking a turn for the better, Carla's sister, who lived on Martha's Vineyard, had asked Carla to come stay with her. Her husband had left her, and she didn't want to be alone.

Carla had subtly suggested Sam should join her on the trip, but he had been so preoccupied with a case he didn't get the hints. Only in hindsight did he realize what she'd been asking. So here he was, either making a grand romantic gesture or a boneheaded impulsive mistake.

"Here goes nothing," he muttered to himself as he flagged down the lone cab waiting outside the ferry terminal.

3

As Sam's cab pulled into the driveway, he saw a woman emerge from the dark red farmhouse. He recognized her from pictures as Vanessa Mayhew, Carla's sister.

The woman ran toward the cab with a panicked, worried look on her face. The driver raised a hand off the steering wheel in a casual wave but she didn't even notice. Sam realized she was trying to see who was in the back seat. When she got close enough to the passenger door where she could see inside the cab clearly, her expression immediately melted into disappointment.

"Hey, Vanessa," the driver said cheerily through the open car windows, completely ignoring the woman's urgent mood.

The words were enough to break the woman out of her trance. She looked at the driver then back at Sam, clearly confused at the unexplained appearance of this stranger in her driveway.

Vanessa Mayhew had a slight build and was average height. Her large, almond eyes were red and puffy from crying. She had the same high cheekbones and full lips as Carla, but with little or no makeup and short, brown hair parted on the side, she had a more natural - even plain - beauty.

Sam waved meekly at the woman staring back at him from outside the car.

"I'm guessing you're Vanessa," he said with a grin.

She literally took a step back upon hearing her name uttered by this stranger.

"Do I know you?" she asked.

Before Sam could answer, Carla opened the front screen door and stepped out on to the porch.

"Sam?" she asked, stunned.

"Oh, this is fun," the driver said with a chuckle.

But Sam barely heard him. His stomach was doing jumping jacks at the sight of his girlfriend. Carla was tall and lean and seemed younger than her 38 years. Her long, dark hair fell casually over her shoulders and she seemed more beautiful than ever.

Sam was used to seeing her with her hair pulled back, the way she wore it at her job as the Hubbard County Medical Examiner. It could almost look severe and definitely intimidating, which was probably Carla's intent. But while she definitely looked softer with her hair down, he could tell from the tired look in her eyes she hadn't been getting much sleep.

"What the hell?" she said as she walked toward the car, just as confused as her sister had been moments earlier. "What are you doing here?"

Sam took a deep breath. "Wish me luck," he mumbled to the driver as he opened the cab door.

"If you don't want me here, just say the word," Sam said as he stepped out of the cab. "I just thought..."

Carla interrupted, throwing her arms around his six-foot frame.

"I can't believe you're here," she said, then pulled back quickly. "Is everything okay?"

Sam smiled. "It is now."

Carla looked in his eyes, still in a state of disbelief but clearly happy.

"Looks like it's safe for me to leave," the driver laughed from inside the car. "Bye, Vanessa."

Vanessa, seeming to notice the driver for the first time, waved in recognition as the cab drove off. Carla turned toward her sister.

"Nessie, this is Sam!"

It all seemed to click in place, and Vanessa finally put the puzzle together.

"You're Sam?"

Sam smiled at Vanessa and reached out his hand to shake hers. He was stunned to see she was not sharing in the enthusiasm. In fact, her face had gone white and her expression was as somber as her words.

"You're here about Norm, aren't you?"

4

SAM THANKED CARLA FOR THE GLASS OF ICE WATER, EVEN though he wished it was something much stronger. His surprise visit and impromptu vacation had quickly taken a turn.

It took a good fifteen minutes to convince Vanessa that a homicide detective showing up at her door had nothing to do with her missing husband. Looking at it from her perspective, Sam could see how she could get the wrong idea. Her husband, Norm, had left in a huff over a week ago and still hadn't returned. When Vanessa realized the man that showed up on her doorstep was Carla's Sam, someone she knew was a detective, she had understandably skipped over the, *Aww, he came to see my sister* reaction and dove head first into the *They think my husband has been murdered* pool.

Vanessa's home was nestled well off the beaten path in Chilmark, a charming rural village on the west side of the island. Sitting on her back deck, the three of them were enjoying the picturesque view of rolling hills and green pastures traced with stone fences. It was what Sam imagined an Irish countryside would look like.

And then there was the ocean. Sitting just past the meadows, about a half mile away, he could see the deep blue waters forming the horizon. A brilliant blue sky sat in contrast above.

"Man, this is gorgeous," Sam said. "Except for that slice of blue ocean out there, it's a lot more country than I expected. I dig it."

An ocean breeze wafted over them and Sam leaned back to take it all in, but Vanessa wasn't very interested in Sam's R&R. Now that she knew Sam was here to visit, she realized she had the ear of a detective and was going to take full advantage.

In a frantic yet hushed voice, she told Sam how she and Norm had had a big fight just over a week ago. She paused, waiting for Sam to ask what the fight was about. But Sam was enjoying the warm sun and cool breeze too much to take the hint.

Realizing he wasn't going to ask, she continued. They were fighting about new equipment for Norm's fishing boat. Norm was a commercial fisherman. Spring was generally fluke season and it brought in a steady income. But this year, Norm had been approached by some of the younger fisherman about raising - and later harvesting - blue mussels. If it worked out, it could be a steady source of income year-round. Norm had taken a significant chunk of their savings to invest in it—without consulting with Vanessa first.

"It's probably a good investment," Vanessa admitted. "I'm sure it is. But it's the fact that he did it without asking me. That's our nest egg. He can't do that."

Not wanting to get caught up in that squabble, Sam nodded and sipped his water.

"Yeah," he said. "I can see how that could get you riled up."

"He was just as riled up as me," Vanessa said defensively. "He got all defensive and started twisting my words. Anyway, it was a doozy of a fight. One of our worst."

Carla had already told him that they fought regularly. He wondered where this last fight fell on the Mayhew Fight Meter.

"He got mad and stormed out, like he always does," she continued. "And I went to bed. Like I always do."

"But when he didn't come home..." Sam said, helping her get to the end of her story.

"Sometimes he takes off for a day or two," Vanessa said. "Just goes out on his boat. Or stays with some friends on the Cape. But a few days went by and he didn't come back. And he didn't take his boat. And his friends never saw him."

Carla sat down next to Sam and put her hand on his knee. He looked at her to see if she was annoyed at her sister hogging his time. But instead, he saw a sincere concern in Carla's eyes. While he had been fully prepared to take off his detective hat for a few days and devote his attention to Carla, he got the sense she wanted him to help as much as Vanessa did. He sat up to listen more intently.

"What did the police say?" he asked.

Vanessa scoffed. "They just think it's Norm being Norm. But this is different. I can tell. I'm really worried. By now, he would have at least called."

At that moment, there was the unmistakable creaking sound of a door opening. It startled Vanessa and she jumped up.

"Hello?" a male voice yelled out from inside the house.

5

VANESSA LET OUT A SIGH OF RECOGNITION WHEN SHE HEARD THE voice.

"We're out here," she yelled into the house then turned to Sam.

"It's Jude," she explained. "My father-in-law. He's also my partner with the lavender farm."

Sam stood to greet a tall man in his early 60s. He was sturdy and solid and his receding salt and pepper hair was cut short so it blended right into his stubbly beard. From his weathered and tanned skin, it was clear to Sam that he lived his life outdoors.

Jude saw Sam, then looked at Vanessa. Sensing his confusion, Sam jumped in, extending his hand.

"Sam Lawson," he said. "I'm Carla's...I know Carla."

He hated describing himself as a boyfriend. It felt so high schoolish. But he didn't know what else to say. Friend sold their relationship short. And he sure as hell wasn't going to say he was Carla's lover.

"He's my boyfriend," Carla chimed in.

Hearing her say it out loud took Sam by surprise. He liked the way it sounded when she said it.

Jude shook Sam's hand. His grip was strong and purposeful.

This guy's a real man's man, Sam thought, unconsciously puffing up his chest a little.

"You're the Texas cop," Jude said. "You might come in handy around here."

"I'll definitely do what I can," Sam answered.

Jude nodded and turned his attention to Vanessa.

"I need to go over some inventory before I head to the store," he said to her.

Vanessa nodded and led Jude back inside. Sam turned to Carla. It was the first time they'd been alone since his arrival, and he suddenly found himself at a loss for words. Carla reached over and squeezed his hand.

"I can't believe you're really here."

"Hope it's okay," Sam said. "I mean, I know you told me I could, but I hope you weren't just saying that to be polite and I showed up anyway and now I've made a total ass out of myself but you can't tell me because you're way too polite."

"I asked you because I wanted you to come," she said.

She shifted in her chair.

"I've done a lot of thinking the last few days," she said gently. "About us."

"Uh oh," Sam said. "Here it comes."

After about six months of dealing with his impulsive, never-a-dull-moment lifestyle, Carla honestly didn't know if she could handle the stress of it all and had put things on hold. But she soon realized their relationship was too important to at least not try to make it work.

"I don't want to lose you, Sam," she said.

Sam's shoulders relaxed and he grinned. "Good thing. Because I'm harder to get rid of than dog crap on a boot."

Carla shook her head and laughed.

"I just wasn't prepared for you coming here," she said. "I really didn't think you would."

"I knew this was a mistake," Sam sighed.

"No," she assured him. "It was a wonderful idea. It's just... my sister is kind of high maintenance right now. She needs a lot of my attention."

"No problem," Sam said. "You do what you gotta do. I'll just enjoy a little vacation. Sleep in late. Sneak away. You won't even know I'm here."

"That's the thing," she said. "I don't know if you noticed or not, but this is a small house."

"Great view, though," he countered.

"It's a one bedroom. I've been sleeping on the couch," she said.

She looked at Sam and waited for him to fill in the dots. He finally did.

"So, you're saying there's no room in the inn."

"We'll figure something out," Carla offered.

Sam kissed her on the forehead.

"I'll sleep in my car," he said. "Except I, uh, don't have a car here."

Carla laughed.

"There's a room in the back," she said. "There's so much junk, you can't even walk through it. But this will be a good excuse to clean it out."

"I heard that," Vanessa said, walking back out on the porch with Jude.

"You keep talking about cleaning it up," Carla said. "You don't have to do a thing. Sam and I will do it."

"There's still the issue of a bed," Vanessa said. "Although I suppose you could get a decent air mattress at the hardware store."

"I've slept on worse," Sam said.

"I'll track down a mattress," Jude offered.

"I appreciate it," Sam said.

Jude nodded back in response.

Vanessa handed a framed photo to Sam.

"This is for you," she said. "That's my Norm. If you're going to find him, you'll need to know what he looks like."

Sam studied the photo of the man sitting on a boat with the sun setting behind him. He looked to be in his mid-40s, with unkempt brown hair and a scruffy beard. His tan skin was weathered by the ocean sun, giving him crow's feet and deep laugh lines that were made even more pronounced by the huge grin on his face.

"He looks pretty happy here," Sam said.

"That's because he's on his boat," Vanessa answered. "That's his baby."

Sam remembered that Vanessa had told him Norm's boat was still in the harbor. So why didn't he take it with him? Probably because he was planning on coming back. Or he left against his will.

6

Jude's rusty brown Ford pickup rolled to a stop at the end of the sandy driveway. He had contacted a family friend who had a spare mattress and the two men had driven over to pick it up.

Sam sat in the passenger seat and looked through the trees at the large Cape Cod home with weathered gray shingle siding and white trim. They had only driven a few miles from Vanessa's house, but the roads were rough and unpaved and Jude had to drive so slow it had taken them nearly twenty minutes to make the quick trip. Sam had tried to pass the time with small talk but Jude wasn't much of a talker. Finally, rather than make another unanswered comment, Sam decided to sit quietly and endure the trek in awkward silence.

Almost feeling suffocated by the silence, Sam jumped out of the truck as soon as it came to a stop.

"Jude?" a woman's voice called out.

Sam spun around, startled, to see a woman in her mid-30s walking toward him from the large house. She was waving at Jude, who was stepping out of the other side of the truck. Sam couldn't help but notice her warm, blue eyes and the way her nose crinkled when she smiled. She had an air of casualness about her that immediately put Sam at ease.

She walked over to Jude and gave him a hug.

"This must be your bedless friend," she said, looking at Sam.

Sam stepped toward her and extended his hand. "I'm Sam Lawson."

She pushed his hand away.

"Sorry, I'm a hugger," she said as she gave Sam a gentle hug. Her body felt soft and Sam took in the fresh, clean scent of her hair.

"I'm Jane Caplan," she said. "But I bet you're more interested in my bed."

Sam stammered, unsure what to say, causing Jane to laugh. She slapped his arm.

"Relax," she said, walking past him toward the house.

Sam looked at Jude, who shrugged his shoulders in response.

Jane pointed to a smaller home across a walkway from her house.

"You're lucky," she said over her shoulder as she walked toward the cottage. "Normally, I've already rented the space out. And the mattress kind of comes with the place. But I haven't had time to clean it out completely."

Sam followed Jane down the thin, sandy path to the cottage. Jane opened the door and sighed with relief.

"Thank God it's open," she said.

They stepped into a small kitchen which opened up into a single large room. It was filled with several paintings in progress. The canvases were either on easels or leaned against the walls. A large wooden cart filled with a huge assortment of tubes of paints sat in the middle of the room.

Jude had told Sam that Jane was an artist and her paintings and sculptures could be found all over town. Sam looked around the room, wondering what pile of paintings were hiding the mattress.

"I put it in the storage room just out back," Jane said, walking through a sliding glass door to the back porch. "I didn't want to get paint all over it."

Jude and Sam followed Jane out the door toward a small storage shed that connected to the cottage. Jane was already at the door, shaking the padlock.

"Oh, shit," she said to herself before turning around red-faced. "I was really hoping I forgot to lock it."

Sam nodded, putting the situation together quickly.

"And you don't have the key," he said.

"I *do* have it," Jane said. "I just don't know where it is. But I will find it. I promise."

She walked back to the two men and led them back into the studio.

"Let me look around," she said. "I'm sure I can find it."

"We could help you look," Sam offered, wanting to speed up the delay.

"Don't be silly," she laughed. "Besides, Lord knows what you'd find if you started digging around. You might get bit."

Jane laughed. It was a soft, earthy laugh.

"I adore your accent," she said. "I can't believe I've got a real Texas cowboy in my studio."

Sam bristled at the stereotype. People always assume that if you're from Texas, then you must be a cowboy. Granted, he was wearing cowboy boots. But that was because they looked cool. Sam had always considered himself more rock-and-roll than country and western. And even though he lived in a smaller city now, he had worked homicide in Houston for over a decade. Still, Jane had said it playfully, so he let it roll off with a smile.

Jude cleared his throat, reminding Jane that he was also in the room.

"Oh, I love the way you talk, too," Jane said to him. "Don't go getting jealous."

Jude started to protest, but Jane was already walking to the door of the studio.

"Here's what I will do," she said. "I've got an air mattress I can loan you. It's got a tiny leak, but it's a decent backup. But I'll probably find my key in no time and I'll text you to come get it. That sound okay?"

Sam nodded. Unless Jude or Vanessa offered another option, it didn't look like he had much of a choice.

"Follow me to the house," she said, as she stepped out the front door of the studio. "I'll get the air mattress and you can give me your phone number."

7

It was late evening as Sam drove up Old Country Road, the main artery that connected Chilmark to the bigger towns of Vineyard Haven and Oak Bluffs.

Vanessa had told Sam that Norm had taken his car when he left, but he also had an old work truck that Sam could borrow while he was on the island. Sam was more than happy to take her up on the generous offer.

The blue '82 Jeep J10 pickup truck had the classic boxy frame and front grill of an old Jeep and the large bed of an old Ford. Its dark blue exterior was accented with patches of rust that only added more character. However, when Sam had opened the door, he was thrown back by the pungent smell of dead fish.

Vanessa had managed a melancholy laugh. "Welcome to the smell of my husband after being out to sea for a couple of days," she said. "Just be thankful it's not late summer."

She assured him the smell was worse than usual because the windows had been rolled up. She suggested he keep the windows open and it would probably air out pretty quick. Sam just hoped the smell wouldn't stick to his clothes. Then again, maybe it would help him fit in as one of the locals.

He was driving to a tavern that Vanessa had recommended. He would rather be spending his first evening on the island with Carla, but she had already promised to take Vanessa to a poetry reading at the Vineyard Haven bookstore. It was something her sister had been looking forward to, and Carla thought the distraction would do her sister good. Anything to get her mind off of her husband's disappearance.

She had invited Sam to come with them, but he had politely declined. He'd sooner get a root canal than listen to someone read poetry for an hour.

Carla had offered that she and her sister could maybe meet up with him later, but Sam could see by the look on Vanessa's face that she had no intention of going to a bar after a night of poetry. So Sam was on his own. The first night of his romantic vacation was going to be spent alone at a bar.

Sam spotted an open barstool and pulled up a seat at the large bar that took up one side of the tavern. He looked around, taking in his surroundings. The main room was narrow, with the bar on one side and a small raised bandstand on the other. While no band was currently playing, a drum set, some electric guitars and some amps were set up, probably for a later show. Behind the bandstand was a half wall - about four feet high - and on the other side of it was a second, larger room with lots of round wooden tables and folding chairs. Sam turned back around to face the bar. He noticed the hand-printed sign with the name of the tavern: THE DIVE IN. Sam smirked. From the cheap furnishings and casual atmosphere, the place more than lived up to its name.

"What can I get you, Hon?" the bartender said in a smoky voice.

Sam ordered a beer and watched as the bartender danced her way to the tap. Probably in her mid to late 40s, she had bleached blonde hair and was dressed in jeans and a ripped black T-shirt that revealed a collection of tattoos on her arms and bare shoulders. She had a badass vibe about her that made Sam think she was either in a heavy metal band or a motorcycle gang.

She brought the beer over to Sam and asked if he wanted to start a tab. Sam handed her a credit card and asked for a menu. The bartender smiled as Sam spoke.

"I know that accent. You're from Texas," she said. "Our first Texan of the season."

Sam nodded and smiled politely.

"Yep," he said sheepishly. "That'd be me."

"First one's on the house, Tex," she said as she tapped the bar with her long black fingernails.

Sam noticed she wore a lot of rings - skulls, crosses and a large silver ring with a shiny black stone. Several black rubber bracelets adorned one wrist and a dainty diamond tennis bracelet graced the other.

"Thank ya kindly, ma'am," Sam said, raising his beer, and pouring his Texas accent on thick.

The bartender motioned for him to wait as she poured herself a beer. They clinked glasses and drank.

"I'm Cicilie," the bartender said. "Most people just call me Cici."

Sam threw back the rest of his beer.

"Nice to meet you, Cici," he said with a smile. "I am ready for another."

Cici nodded in approval and got him a new beer.

"Welcome to The Dive In, Ready-For-Another," she said.

8

JANE TOGGLED THE SWITCH ON THE BACK OF A LARGE HALOGEN
work light and the entire studio lit up like a construction site.

She had spent a good hour looking for the padlock key and
had all but given up hope. She had been getting dressed for a
date when she had a thought that the key could still be in the
studio. When she got in a "painting state", as she liked to call it,
she wouldn't really notice anything else. It was possible that
she had the key in the studio and had sat it down somewhere.

Her fixation on finding the key was fueled partially by feelings of guilt for not delivering on her promise to the nice Texan,
and partly a way to deal with her nervous energy. She needed
to have a serious conversation with her boyfriend and she was
not looking forward to it.

She sifted through canvases as she played out the conversation in her head when something caught her attention from
outside. She looked through the large sliding glass door into
the woods that separated the studio from her house. The sun
had already set, but there was still just enough light to create a
mosaic of shadows among the trees.

Jane squinted to see past the reflection of the large shop light. She slid open the glass door to get a better look.

She stared into the shadows, looking for any sign of movement or life. She could have sworn she saw something.

"Hello?" she called out into the woods. "Anyone there?"

The snap of a branch came from the trees to her right and she spun around. It wasn't unusual to see a small deer this time of year, but Jane's voice would have typically scared them off.

A shadow seemed to move in the distance. Or was it just the trees swaying in the evening breeze? Jane's heart beat faster. Something didn't feel right.

"Who's there?" she demanded, this time more forcibly.

She stepped back into the studio and slowly slid the door shut. The spotlight created such a huge reflection that she couldn't see out, but if anyone was outside, they could clearly see her. She kept walking backwards, not taking her eyes off the door until she reached the light stand. With one hand, she flipped the toggle, turning off the light.

Feeling less exposed, her fear subsided and she rationalized the movement to an animal or the wind. Still, she decided to hold off on looking for the key until tomorrow morning, when there was more light. She wanted to get back to her house before it was completely dark.

She walked back through the studio, using her hand along the walls to guide her. Then, just as she reached the front door, a memory hit her. She smiled and shook her head as she reached up and felt along the top ridge of the door trim. Sure enough, there was the key. Right where she now remembered leaving it. She laughed to herself. It wasn't the first time she had hid something for safekeeping, only to forget where she hid it. If she ever sold her house, Lord knows what treasures the new owners would eventually find.

Fueled by her victory, Jane opened the door to the cottage. And immediately let out a terrifying scream.

A man stood in the shadows less than three feet in front of her. Jane gasped and took a step backwards. The man stepped forward out of the shadows and laughed.

"Holy shit! I scared you to death," he laughed.

It was John Rowe. Jane's boyfriend.

"You asshole!" Jane yelled, trying to catch her breath.

"I'm sorry, Baby," John said, stepping into the studio and reaching out to comfort her. Jane batted him away.

"You enjoyed it," she said, starting to calm down.

John smiled. He knew better than to say anything else. Jane looked at him and eventually smiled. It was hard for her to stay mad at him. John casually ran his fingers through his medium-length brown hair, revealing hazel eyes that were unnervingly intense. In his early 40s, John was tall and lean, with broad shoulders and rugged good looks. He looked good for his age but didn't spend a lot of time on his appearance. He was what he was. Without apology. That's one of the things Jane liked about him.

"Sorry I'm early," he finally said. "Just anxious to see you I guess."

Jane punched him in the arm for good measure and then led him out of the studio, locking the door behind her.

9

SAM SHOOK HIS HEAD.

"I swear to you. I never have," he said.

Cici laughed. "You mean to tell me you've never ever worn a cowboy hat?"

"That's not what you asked," Sam corrected. "You asked if I ever *owned* a cowboy hat."

Cici, along with a couple of other customers, had been playfully teasing Sam about Texas stereotypes.

"So, what? You rent them?" Cici asked.

"Yeah," Sam answered. "When I need one, I just hop on my horse that I keep tied up to the oil well in my backyard."

Ed, an older man sitting four stools down from Sam chimed in.

"I thought you just drove your pickup."

Sam nodded as he gulped down a bite of the burger he had ordered. "That part is true. We do all drive trucks. It's a state law."

Sam always felt at home in a bar, and tonight was no exception. While he would still rather be with Carla, he was slightly relieved when she had texted him that she and her sister were going to grab a quiet dinner at a local restaurant and wouldn't be home for another hour or two. That was just enough time for Sam to catch a little bit of the band before meeting them back at the house. On top of that, Jane had texted him that she had found the key to her storage shed and suggested he come by the next morning to get the mattress.

Considering his work done for the day, Sam turned his attention back to his new friends, who had all turned their attention to the band that had taken the stage.

There were three guys and one woman — all in their 40s and 50s — who looked like they just got off the late shift at a local factory. But they handled their instruments with the confidence of people that had been doing this for a long time. The guitarist, a tall man with short gray hair let loose with a loud, blues riff. The drummer, who looked younger than the rest of the band, adjusted the snare with a series of beats. The woman, looking more like an old-fashioned schoolteacher than a musician, tuned her bass seriously. The guitarist counted to five as he set the volume on the mic, then looked at the bartender.

"We're ready when you are, Your Highness," he said into the mic.

The bar, which had become pretty crowded in the two hours that Sam had been there, erupted in applause. Sam was surprised to see Cici walk around the end of the bar and step up on the bandstand. The guitarist slid the mic stand in front of her and she adjusted it to her height.

"Thanks for coming out tonight to The Dive In," she yelled. "You ready to rock it up?"

The place exploded in cheers again.

"This one's for our new friend, Tex," Cici said, pointing at Sam. He raised his beer glass in appreciation and the band kicked into a rousing version of a ZZ Top song. The band was tight and Cici's voice was raw and soulful. Sam looked over at Ed, who was also getting into the music.

"She's good!" Sam yelled to Ed.

"Don't you know who she is?" Ed yelled back. "That's Cici Kovak."

Sam instantly recognized the name. Cici Kovak was a rocker in the early 80s, kind of a cross between Joan Jett and Chrissie Hynde. She had black hair then, which is probably why Sam didn't recognize her. But he remembered her growling songs and music videos that were half sexy and all attitude. And here she was on stage in front of him. She'd even been serving him drinks! Sam soaked in the whole scene, grinning ear to ear like a kid on Christmas morning. This had turned out to be quite a night. He looked around to see if everyone else was enjoying the show as much as he was and he noticed the something caught his eye out the front door, which was propped open to let in fresh air.

A woman stepped out of a restaurant across the street. Sam immediately recognized her as his mattress benefactor, Jane Caplan. But something wasn't right. She seemed upset. Then a man walked out the door behind her. Jane turned, blocking Sam's view of the man. But from the way Jane was flailing her arms, they were clearly arguing. He could see the man put his hands on Jane's shoulders, as if to try to calm her, but she threw them off.

Out of instinct, Sam stood and headed toward the door to make sure everything was alright. But the bar was packed, and as the crowd moved their way toward the bandstand, it became harder to maneuver through them. Sam slowly pushed his way through, staying focused on the fighting couple. At one point, it looked like Jane was storming off alone, but with so many people blocking his view, it was hard to tell. Finally, he reached the door. He stepped outside, free from the masses and looked around. He was too late. Both Jane and the man were gone.

10

"HEY YOU."

He heard the muffled voice. But something wasn't right.

It sounded far away but also right beside him. He turned his head and the movement stirred him into consciousness. He opened his eyes and found himself face down on the floor. Well, face down on a completely deflated air mattress, to be more exact.

Then he felt a body slide over his back and kiss him on the cheek.

"Good morning," Carla whispered in his ear.

Sam smiled. He shifted on the floor to turn around, his body stiff and sore from the lack of mattress. But his movement also stirred up memories of the night before. Carla had been waiting for him when he arrived home shortly after midnight. He slid under the sheets beside her and they locked in a passionate embrace that soon crumbled into giggles. Trying to keep quiet so as not to wake Vanessa in the next room, they had felt like two kids in their parents' basement.

Carla brought Sam back to the present with a kiss on the forehead.

"I think we killed the mattress," she said with a sly smile.

Sam grinned.

"No regrets," he said, then groaned as he tried to sit up. "Well, maybe a few."

Carla sat up with Sam, the sheet slipping off of her. He leaned into her and kissed her neck, running a hand down her body.

"Want to try it without the mattress?" he asked.

Carla laughed and pushed him away with a kiss.

"I don't want to put you in traction," she teased.

She stood, and Sam marveled at her body. How did he get so lucky to wind up with a woman like this? She was not only gorgeous, but funny, smart and patient. Patient being the key. She somehow tolerated more than most. And Sam knew he was a better man because of her. He also knew he was not going to let her slip through his hands again.

Carla reached out a hand to help Sam stand.

"Come on, Romeo," she said. "Let's get some coffee."

Sam took her hand and rose to his feet with a loud groan of pain. He rolled his shoulders and twisted his torso, trying to work out the kinks. Getting that mattress was definitely a priority today.

Thinking of the mattress reminded him of seeing Jane having a fight the night before. He had told Carla about it and she reminded him that couples fight. Not everything has to be a criminal act.

She turned off the box fan near the far wall and a silence filled the air. Sam didn't realize the fan had been that loud. But that had been the point. Carla had turned it on to drown out the sounds of their lovemaking.

Carla threw on the shirt Sam had worn the night before and left to make coffee while Sam pulled some jeans and a black T-shirt from his duffel and got dressed. When Jane had texted him, she had asked if he could come by before 10:00 as she needed to run errands after that. He glanced at his watch and saw it was already 9:00.

Sam walked down the hallway toward the kitchen, where he could smell the fresh aroma of coffee being made. Framed photos covered the walls, most of them of Vanessa and Norm. Sam studied the images. They seemed to be a happy couple. Most of the photos were of the two of them laughing together, holding hands or in each other's arms. There were a couple of Vanessa and Jude in front of their lavender farm. And a few photos of Norm on his boat. In every picture, Norm was dressed in a T-shirt and wearing either shorts or jeans. What Sam assumed was a large shark's tooth hung from a black cord around his neck. He was barrel-chested and fit, as you would expect of a fisherman. Sam noticed one other common theme in the photos. He was either holding a bottle of beer or there was one sitting beside him.

Carla walked up behind him.

"Seems to be quite the party guy," Sam said.

"He does enjoy life," Carla said.

"Live hard. Party harder," Sam said. "I like him already."

Carla took Sam's hand and led him into the kitchen.

"I don't want to wake her up," she said, pointing toward Vanessa's bedroom door.

Sam smiled and pulled Carla close to him.

"She's probably exhausted," he joked. "I bet we kept her up all night."

"She's been taking sleeping pills, idiot," Carla replied. "This whole thing with Norm has really been hard on her."

They took their coffee out on the deck. The morning sky was already a brilliant blue and the ocean sparkled in the distance. Sam enjoyed the view as he told Carla about his plans to search for Norm. Maybe ask around the docks where Norm kept his boat. Visit the local police to find out what they knew.

"But first, I promised this woman I would come pick up the mattress by 10:00," Sam said. "You wanna come?"

"I insist," Carla replied. "I need to meet the lady who was trying to get my man in bed."

Sam was shocked she knew about that. Carla saw the surprise on his face.

"I know all," Carla teased. "Never forget it."

Sam laughed. He watched as Carla walked back down the hall to get dressed, then he stepped out on the deck, shivering in the cool morning air and taking in the gorgeous view. It was looking to be another beautiful day and Sam couldn't help but smile.

11

S̲ᴀᴍ ᴋɴᴏᴄᴋᴇᴅ ᴏɴ ᴛʜᴇ ᴡʜɪᴛᴇ ᴅᴏᴏʀ ᴏꜰ ᴛʜᴇ ɢʀᴀʏ Cᴀᴘᴇ Cᴏᴅ home.

"Hopefully, she hasn't lost it again," Sam joked. "And I have to warn you. She may not be too happy to meet you. I think she's got the hots for me."

Carla laughed. "Why does every man think if a woman is even halfway nice they must have the hots for them?"

"Don't forget," Sam replied. "I'm a detective. I'm trained to pick up on personal cues."

He knocked on the door again.

"Maybe she's out back," Sam said. "Do you mind?"

Carla picked up on Sam's concern and followed him around to the side of the house. As they walked past the sweet scent of a thick iris bush, they craned their necks to look over it into a window. Lights were clearly on inside but, from their angle, it was hard to make out more than that. Sam continued toward the backyard, but something in the window caught Carla's eye. She pushed forward into the bush to get a closer look.

"Sam," Carla muttered, beckoning him back.

Sam walked back to her and maneuvered around the large

plant so he could look in the window better. It appeared to be a small dining room with very few furnishings. Four chairs surrounded a round farm table and there was also something on the floor behind it. He cupped his hands on the window to block off the reflection of the clear blue sky.

Sam scooted along the window to get a look from a different angle.

"Holy shit," he muttered.

It was a body lying on the floor in a pool of blood.

12

JANE'S FRONT YARD WAS OVERRUN BY VEHICLES, INCLUDING AN ambulance and a barrage of police cars from Chilmark, as well as the towns of West Tisbury, Oak Bluffs and Edgartown.

After spotting the body, Sam ran to the front of the house and found the front door unlocked. They both rushed inside and were shocked to find Jane's bloodied body. Carla had called 911 immediately, and Sam started looking for signs of a killer.

By the time the cops had shown up, they were both waiting outside so as not to disturb the crime scene. An hour later, they were still there, leaning against the trunk of one of the squad cars when Sam spotted a man emerging from the house. The man was clean-cut with boyish good looks that made him look much younger than he probably was. He had short, light brown hair, blue eyes and a wrestler's body - muscular and compact. He wasn't in uniform but was clearly a cop - probably the acting detective. And from the swagger in his walk, Sam guessed a very cocky one at that.

Sam beelined it toward the detective, leaving Carla and the uniformed officer mid-statement. He extended his hand as he approached.

"Hey, I'm guessing you're the man in charge," Sam said. "I'm Detective Sam Lawson. I called this in."

The detective threw a perplexed look at Sam.

"You're a detective where?" he asked.

"Oh, not here," Sam said with a chuckle. "Back in Texas. I'm here visiting."

The detective looked back at Carla where Sam was pointing.

"And you were here, why?" he asked.

"I was going to borrow a mattress," Sam said. "I came by yesterday. With Jude Mayhew? But the victim here couldn't find the key to the storage shed."

"So you came back this morning," the detective said.

"She texted me last night," Sam said, reaching into his pocket to get his phone.

"You see anything out of the ordinary this morning?" the detective asked.

"Other than a dead, bloody body? No."

Turner looked at Sam, clearly not amused at his attempt at humor.

"I didn't get your name," Sam said, switching topics.

"Detective Turner," he answered. "And as a fellow detective, you have to appreciate all I have going on here, so if you'll excuse me."

Turner tried to walk past Sam, but Sam wasn't ready to end the conversation.

"I told one of the uniforms that there didn't appear to be any signs of forced entry," Sam said. "And no real sign of a struggle. At least, up until the point of attack. My girlfriend is a medical examiner and she..."

"An M.E., seriously? Are you two a traveling murder squad?" Turner asked, his patience clearly running thin.

"Hey, I'm just trying to help," Sam said, slightly stunned at the detective's attitude.

"I appreciate it. But we've got it under control," Turner said.

"I saw her last night in town," Sam offered. "She was having an argument with someone."

"You saw Jane in town last night?" Turner asked. "You seemed to see a lot of Miss Caplan."

"Listen, pal. A lady was murdered and I'm trying to help. You don't need to cop an attitude," he stopped and cracked a sly smile. "Cop an attitude. I didn't even mean to do that."

Turner did not share in the amusement.

"A woman is dead, sir," Turner reminded him. "Maybe that's something you take lightly in Texas, but we take it very seriously. Now if you'll excuse me."

Sam nodded.

"Sorry," he said. "You're right. But if there's anything I can do to help..."

"Do you know how many vacationing cops we get here that are just trying to help? And it's not even Memorial Day yet," Turner said. "The way you can help the most is by letting us do our job."

He walked past Sam, purposefully brushing his shoulder.

"Oh, and I'm going to need you and your medical examiner girlfriend to come to the station," he yelled back over his shoulder. "I'll need a fresh set of fingerprints to check against the ones we found in the house."

Sam waved back at him in acknowledgement, his fingers bent ever so slightly to subtly flip the detective off.

13

SAM SAT AT A SMALL TABLE IN WHAT WAS DOUBLING AS AN interrogation room at the Chilmark Police Station. It was actually a conference room separated by a glass wall from the rest of the station. Sam impatiently drummed his fingers on the table as he looked out at the cluster of cops that were maneuvering around the row of desks in the small space. Carla, who was sitting impatiently at one of the desks, looked over at him and Sam waved with exaggerated enthusiasm.

When Sam and Carla arrived at the station, Sam had noticed a nameplate on the desk where Carla was now sitting: Sgt. Det. Paul Turner.

Well, at least he has a first name, Sam thought.

Growing restless, Sam stood in hope of finding his new detective friend in the crowd of cops. At that moment, Turner appeared around the corner and walked in the conference room, shutting the door behind him.

"So, Detective Sam Lawson," he said. "You've made quite a name for yourself down in Texas."

"You know how it is," Sam said with mock humility. "Seems like I'm always at the right place at the right time."

"Like you were this morning, huh?" Turner asked.

Before Sam could even protest, Turner started laughing.

"I'm just busting your chops," he said with a smile.

He sat down on the other side of the table from Sam.

"So you've got a legit team back in Texas, right?" Turner asked. "I mean, we're a skeleton crew. Not much need for more than that normally."

"Consider yourself lucky," Sam said. "Less people means less red tape."

While it seemed the detective was warming up, Sam kept his guard up. It wouldn't make sense for such an abrupt change in attitude.

Don't bullshit a bullshitter, Sam thought to himself.

"So, as I said earlier," Sam said, changing the subject. "Last night I saw the victim in an argument with someone. I couldn't make out who it was, but I know the restaurant they were at so it would be easy..."

"It was her boyfriend," Turner interrupted. "We already checked it out."

"So, I'm guessing you're bringing him in for questioning, right?"

Turner laughed, shaking his head.

"I said I have a skeleton crew," Turner said. "But I assure you, I know what I'm doing."

"I was just asking," Sam said. "Didn't mean to offend."

"I know these people. You don't," Turner said. "Trust me. It was just a little lover's quarrel."

"You and I both know the boyfriend is always the first suspect," Sam said. "Except for the husband. It's the husband and then the boyfriend. Unless there's both. Then I guess it's a toss-up."

Turner listened impatiently, waiting for him to finish.

"Boyfriend's name is John Rowe. I've known him my whole

life, detective," Turner said. "He's a good friend. Not that I owe you any explanation, but I can assure you he is not a murderer. Especially one as brutal as this one. Stabbed fifteen times."

"Guess that's what they mean by overkill," Sam said with a smirk.

Turner shook his head in disapproval.

"Oh, come on," Sam protested. "That was funny! It's gallows humor. It's what we cops do."

"I knew the victim, detective," Turner said. "I don't find any of this funny."

Sam felt ashamed. He had forgotten this was a small, tight-knit community. And he was being a loudmouth Texas asshole.

"I'm sorry," he said. "That was out of line. Nervous habit."

Turner nodded and sat down across from Sam. He seemed to be deciding how much he could share with this visiting cop.

"Any luck with fingerprints?" Sam asked, once again changing the subject.

Turner welcomed the detour.

"The place had been wiped clean," Turner said. "We didn't even find any of Jane's prints near the crime scene. Just you, your examiner friend and one other that we're trying to match."

"Why would someone go to all the trouble to wipe the place down and then leave a set of prints?" Sam asked.

Turner shrugged. "Got nervous? Got sloppy? Who knows?"

"That's got to seem a little fishy to you," Sam said.

Before Turner could answer, a uniformed officer entered the room and handed a file to Turner. Turner tried to keep a poker face, but Sam noted a hint of surprise.

"Put this on my desk, please," Turner said to the officer.

Turner pulled out his phone and turned his back to Sam, speaking in muffled tones. Sam looked out through the glass wall and got Carla's attention, motioning at the file that had just been set down on the desk in front of her. Carla, getting the hint, discreetly opened the file and began to read. Turner hung up the phone, but just before he turned around, Sam saw Carla gasp in shock.

14

"AND YOU'RE SURE YOU READ IT RIGHT?" SAM ASKED AS HE PACED back and forth in Vanessa's living room.

"I know how to read a report," Carla replied. "I write them, remember?"

Sam held up his hands in surrender.

"I'm sorry," he said.

Carla grabbed Sam's hand as he paced by her, stopping him. He looked at her and smiled.

"Maybe they were old prints," Vanessa offered.

Carla turned to her sister, who was sitting next to her on the couch.

"Let's hope," Carla said. "But right now, all we know is that Norm's fingerprints were found at the scene of the crime. And they were the only prints besides the two of us. Luckily, from what I could read, they got them from LED light, which means they probably weren't visible to the naked eye."

"Right," Sam chimed in. "Because that means... What does it mean?"

"It means it wasn't a bloody fingerprint or something truly incriminating," Carla explained.

"Would Norm have had a reason to visit Jane?" Sam asked.

Vanessa shook her head.

"I don't know," she said. "He may have done some yard work for her or something? He did all kinds of odd jobs for people during the off-season."

"Any reason why he would have been there recently?" Sam asked, treading carefully. "Like, last night?"

Vanessa looked at Sam in shock. "What are you saying?"

"They'll probably send the prints out for analysis to get a better idea of how old they were," Carla interrupted, changing the subject.

"They can do that?" Vanessa asked.

Carla nodded with a shrug. "Science."

"It won't matter," Vanessa blurted. "Paul Turner has had it out for Norm for years. And Norm doesn't help matters."

"Doesn't help how?" Sam asked.

"He drinks too much. Gets into bar fights," Vanessa explained. "But all little stuff. Nothing like this. Norm would never kill anyone."

"Luckily, the worst Turner can do is arrest him," Sam said. "If he doesn't have a case, it won't stand up in court."

"He'll build a case," Vanessa said. "Even if he has to make it up."

She looked up at Sam, her eyes pleading.

"You need to prove he's innocent," she said.

"It's kinda hard to do that with him missing," Sam said.

"Then you need to find him," Vanessa said. "Or find the real killer."

"You have police here to do that," Sam said.

"It couldn't hurt if you helped, could it?" Vanessa asked. "I need to know someone is on Norm's side."

Sam looked at Carla, unsure what to say.

"You know anyone who would have wanted Jane dead?" Sam asked.

Vanessa seemed surprised by the question.

"I didn't know her that well," she answered. "But she had a way of making enemies."

15

VANESSA'S HANDS TREMBLED AS SHE LOADED THE TRAY OF lavender cuttings on to the back of her all-terrain vehicle. Too nervous and upset to sit at home while Sam and Carla went in search of Norm, she decided to catch up on some work at Vineyard Lavender, the lavender farm she ran with her father-in-law, Jude.

Jude had been doing most of the manual labor this spring, especially since Norm's disappearance. Even though he was in his 60s, he was more than able to handle the physically demanding work and he delegated anything he couldn't handle to a small group of seasonal workers.

Even though most of the planting had already been done, Vanessa had found a few more cuttings in the greenhouse and was loading up the ATV when Jude stepped inside.

"You need any help?" he offered gently.

Vanessa shook her head, mustering as much energy as she could to appear brave.

"I've got most of the new cuttings planted," Jude continued, pretending not to notice Vanessa's fragile state.

He had just returned from the police station, where he had

given a statement on his visit to Jane's house the day before. They had also asked if he had any information on Norm's whereabouts, which he didn't. Jude and Norm had never really got along well and, in recent months, if they did talk, it was with raised voices. If Jude hadn't been in business with Vanessa, the father and son would probably never speak.

Now, with his son not only missing but also wanted for questioning in a murder investigation, Jude grew even more resentful of the pain his son was putting everyone through. Particularly Vanessa.

He and Vanessa had clicked almost immediately. Norm was an only child and Vanessa quickly became the daughter Jude never had. His wife, Norm's mother, had died of breast cancer when Norm was still just a kid. Jude had never remarried and had no interest in other women. But Vanessa filled a maternal void in both men's lives. When Vanessa had come to him with the proposal to start a lavender farm on the island, Jude jumped at the opportunity. Norm was happy for his wife, but never hid his resentment for his father backing her dreams while always turning a cold shoulder to his only son's requests. But Jude felt he could trust Vanessa, and it was a sound business plan. Norm, on the other hand, never thought things through and had the shoddy track record to prove it.

"If you'd like, I could drive those out for you," Jude said to Vanessa.

"I just need to keep busy," Vanessa finally spoke. "If you don't mind."

"Of course not," Jude said.

He turned to leave but hesitated at the greenhouse door.

"If you need to talk," he said, "I'm here."

Vanessa smiled at him. She knew that listening to someone's feelings would be the last thing Jude would ever want to do. But that made the offer mean so much more to her.

As Jude left her in the greenhouse, Vanessa finished loading up the ATV and opened the side door to drive out. As she pushed it forward, the handle poked her forearm and she winced at the pain. She pulled back her shirt sleeve to check the bandage it had covered. Peeling the medical tape back, she lifted the bandage to look at the large cut underneath. Relieved that she hadn't re-opened the wound, she re-applied the bandage and rolled her sleeve back down to cover it.

16

THE HOSPITAL ROOM WAS BUSTLING WITH PARAMEDICS, DOCTORS, police officers and a couple of Coast Guard officers. Martha's Vineyard Hospital didn't have a morgue, so the medical staff and law enforcement teams were preparing for the Coast Guard to transport the body across the sound to Woods Hole. There was so much chaos in the room that no one even noticed Carla slip in.

She maneuvered through the throngs toward the hospital bed that was serving as the temporary home of Jane's body. Much to her dismay, however, the body was still encased in a black body bag.

"Excuse me," a man said to Carla, grabbing her arm. "Who are you?"

Carla turned to face a tall, slim man in his mid-40s with close-cropped hair as white as snow. Carla waved her medical examiner badge quickly in front of the man's face.

"I'm a medical examiner," she blurted. "Just wanted to take a quick look."

"Like hell you are," the man said, tightening his grip on the Carla's arm. "Who let this woman in here?"

"I *am* a medical examiner," Carla explained. "I'm just..."

"Do you people have no shame?" the man asked.

A police officer stepped forward to help.

"Can you keep the press out of here?" the white-haired man snapped to the officer.

But before he could haul Carla out of the room, Detective Turner stepped forward.

"She's not with the press," he said, looking Carla dead in the eyes. "But she still shouldn't be here."

"Detective, I came to offer my services," Carla said. "I know you don't have an M.E. on the island."

"Doctor Vincent is our county M.E.," Turner said, pointing at the white-haired man. "We're transporting the body over to his office in Woods Hole now."

"But that's on Cape Cod," Carla said.

"That's why the Coast Guard is here," Turner replied back. "Now I appreciate all of this southern hospitality, but you and your boyfriend need to let us do our jobs. Believe it or not, we are more than capable."

They were distracted by the crash of metal instruments behind them. A woman had stepped backwards into a tray of equipment, toppling it on its side.

"Nurse! Would you pay attention?" the white-haired doctor yelled.

The petite nurse shrunk back into the wall, her big doe eyes red and swollen from tears. Turner stepped between the red-faced doctor and the nurse.

"Come on, Doc. Take it easy," he said.

"Oh. Are you going to get in my way, too?" the doctor yelled indignantly. "I have a body to move!"

"That 'body' was her best friend," Turner snapped back. "So you're going to need to cut her a little slack."

Carla looked over at the nurse and realized the tears weren't from embarrassment, but from grief.

"Well, if she's her best friend, she's going to want to let me do my job so I can help find her killer," the doctor snapped back at Turner before shifting his glare to the nurse. "Will that work for you?"

The nurse nodded her head, trying to stay as stoically professional as possible. Carla stepped back as the medical team transferred Jane's body from the hospital bed to a gurney. Clearly, she wasn't going to get a chance to do her own examination. She watched the nurse help the Coast Guard officers wheel the gurney out of the room while Dr. Vincent bellowed demands at anyone who would listen.

As the nurse passed her, she looked up and the two women locked eyes. The poor nurse seemed to be barely holding it together, and Carla's heart broke for her. But she knew she'd need to talk to her. Her stomach did somersaults. Carla was more comfortable examining bodies than interrogating witnesses. But if she was going to help, she needed to step out of her comfort zone.

Carla took a deep breath and followed the medical team, but was pulled back when someone grabbed her arm.

17

Sam pulled the Jeep into the driveway and stepped out. Either keeping the windows rolled down was actually helping to get rid of the fish smell or Sam was getting used to it. Either way, it wasn't bothering him as much, so he was happy. Besides, if you're going to smell like fish, might as well be in a fishing village.

He had come back to Vanessa's house after a second trip to the police station. He had hoped some of the other officers would be willing to offer him some information about the case, but they all had been as distrustful of an outsider as Turner. Not that Sam blamed him. He'd be the same way if some tourist detective walked into his station and demanded information on a case he was working on.

Carla and her sister were gone but Sam recognized Jude's truck in the driveway. He let himself in the house and yelled out for him, but there was no answer. Figuring he was probably out in the large garage barn behind the house, Sam opened the refrigerator door and stared inside, foraging around for something to snack on.

He was distracted by an odd noise on the back deck. The

curtains to the sliding glass door had been drawn overnight, so, after grabbing an apple, Sam walked across the living room to open them. He yanked back the curtain and stared into the face of an older man. Letting out a yell, he dropped the apple and as he stepped backwards, tripped on it.

As he toppled to the floor, he realized the man was Jude.

"Oh, good," Jude said, stepping inside and ignoring what had just happened. "I was hoping to find you."

Sam picked up the apple and scurried to his feet.

"Damn apple," he said, making an excuse.

Jude walked past him, shaking his head. Sam wasn't sure if it was in disbelief or disgust.

He followed the old man into the kitchen, feeling an odd need to try to impress Jude.

"You know Vanessa is my daughter-in-law," Jude said, sitting down at the table. "She's actually more like a daughter."

"Is that because Norm is your son?" Sam joked.

From the lack of response, Sam quickly realized that fun time was over.

"Vanessa's responsible," Jude said. "Norm *tries* to do the right thing."

"I see there how you emphasized the word *tries*," Sam asked.

"He doesn't think. He's too impulsive. Like a kid," Jude continued. "And he keeps pulling Vanessa down with him. I don't like that. Norm can take care of himself. I taught him that much. But Vanessa shouldn't have to pay the price for Norm's shortcomings."

"You think he killed Jane?" Sam asked, cutting to the chase.

Jude stared at the Texas lawman in front of him.

"I can tell you one thing. He's not a killer," Jude answered. "But if he did it, I'll be the first to help bring him in. The law is the law. I just need you to know that he's not a killer. Because I don't know if Paul Turner believes that."

He explained that Turner and Norm had a long-standing feud. Even in high school they were rivals. Whether it was sports or girls, they were always at odds.

"Paul's a good cop," Jude said. "But we don't get a lot of murders on the island. And he's way too proud to ever admit he's in over his head."

"I already told Vanessa I'd help find out who did this," Sam said.

"I know," Jude said as he stood up from the table. "Come with me."

They walked out the front door to Jude's pickup, and Jude pulled a silver metal box from the passenger seat.

"What's this?" Sam said as Jude handed it to him.

"Portable police scanner that hooks up in your car," Jude answered. "Paul's not going to tell you what's going on. You're going to have to find out on your own."

18

CARLA HAD RETURNED TO VANESSA'S HOME SLIGHTLY DEFLATED. When she had tried to follow the nurse, Detective Turner had grabbed her arm to stop her. He chided her for interfering and made sure she was escorted back to her car before she could even get the nurse's name. She complied, knowing she could go back at a later time easily enough. Then she decided the easiest thing to do would be to ask her sister.

Vanessa was sitting on the back porch with a glass of white wine and staring off at the ocean in the distance. After planting the lavender cuttings, she had surveyed the farm but realized Jude had everything under control. With no actual work to do, she returned home. She might as well enjoy an afternoon drink.

Carla walked on to the back porch, noticing the wine glass in her sister's hand.

"Starting early today?" she asked.

"Hey, I waited until the afternoon," Vanessa answered.

Carla revealed a wine glass that she had brought outside with her.

"That's good enough for me," she said with a smile.

Vanessa grabbed the bottle of Pinot Grigio next to her chair and poured a glass for her younger sister.

"How did it go with the medical examiner?" she asked.

Carla filled her in on the chaos at the hospital and the status of Jane's body. She then asked her sister about the nurse who claimed to be Jane's best friend. Vanessa nodded.

"That would have to be Gina Moffet," she said. "Although best friend might be stretching it."

"Why do you say that?" Carla asked.

Vanessa thought about her answer and then shrugged her shoulders.

"You know what? For all I know, she could be her best friend," she said.

She explained that she knew Gina in passing, but that was about it.

"She lives and works in Oak Bluffs," Vanessa explained. "I tend to stay up island as much as I can."

"But Jane lives around here," Carla said.

"Jane is much more of a social creature than I am," Vanessa said with a laugh before suddenly growing somber. "Was."

She suddenly spun around in her seat and faced Carla.

"You don't think Norm did it, do you?" she asked.

Carla squeezed her sister's hands. "Of course not," she answered.

She hoped her sister didn't notice the slight hesitation in her voice. But Carla barely knew Norm. She didn't know what he was or wasn't capable of. She had been involved with too many murder cases where the attacker turned out being the one everyone suspected least. She had learned to keep an open mind until there was conclusive evidence.

"Do you think Sam can find the real killer?" Vanessa asked.

Carla smiled proudly. "I have no doubt," she said. "He's a better cop than he even realizes."

"I just have to believe he showed up here for a reason," Vanessa said.

Carla laughed. "Uh, yeah. He showed up here for me."

The two women laughed until it settled into a comfortable silence.

"Can I tell you something?" Vanessa finally asked.

Carla turned to her sister and nodded.

Vanessa's voice cracked as she spoke.

"I don't know if I'm sure Norm didn't do it."

19

THE NEXT MORNING, SAM DROVE TO MENEMSHA HARBOR TO check out Norm's boat. He yawned, still exhausted from the day before. He had spent the evening with Carla and her sister, trying to calm her about the police's suspicion of Norm. He had explained that police investigations can be more about eliminating suspects than zeroing in on them, and that the police just wanted to remove his name from the list.

That was a lie, of course. In reality, Detective Turner considered Norm his primary suspect and Sam feared he wasn't staying open to other possibilities. It made it even more important to find Norm fast. And hopefully he would have a good alibi for where he was the night of the murder.

Carla had also told Sam about Vanessa's uncertainty about her husband's innocence. But by the time he had got back to the house, she seemed to have buried those suspicions and was once again steadfastly certain of his innocence. Still, something had caused that lapse in belief and he hoped Carla could get it out of her.

Sam pulled into the parking lot of Menemsha Harbor. The 300-year-old fishing port looked exactly the way Sam imagined an old fishing harbor would. The first thing he noticed was the row of gray shingled shacks that backed up to a wooden dock lined with various fishing vessels. The rest of the harbor was filled with a wide range of boats: from shiny, new luxury sailboats to beat-up commercial fishing vessels. While it had become a bit of a tourist attraction, especially because of the beautiful sunsets seen from the adjoining beach, it was still a working harbor and the hub for many of the island's local fishermen, including Norm Mayhew.

Sam parked Norm's work truck in the lot at the end of the harbor and walked toward the small building at the dock's edge. The gas pump in front of it led Sam to believe it was a place where he could find someone in charge. As he got closer, the word HARBORMASTER scrawled in red paint above the door confirmed his instincts. Just as he grabbed the door handle a deep baritone voice called out from further down the dock.

"I'll be right there," the man shouted.

Sam looked down the harbor and a portly man in a dark blue windbreaker waved as he walked toward him, clearly in no hurry. When he turned to yell something to a fisherman behind him, Sam noticed the word HARBORMASTER in white letters across the back of the windbreaker.

"Door's locked," the man said as he got closer to Sam. "Already been that kind of morning."

Sam laughed, and the man shook his hand, introducing himself as Dan Mondrick. Sam gave his name and a quick flash of his badge, telling the harbormaster he was helping Detective Turner with the Jane Caplan murder. At the mention of her name, Mondrick's round face became somber.

"That just breaks my heart about her," he said. "She was a good lady."

"I was hoping you could let me take a look at Norm Mayhew's boat," Sam said.

Mondrick sighed. "I keep telling you boys that you're barking up the wrong tree with Norm," he said. "He's not a killer."

The harbormaster pointed at a boat docked on the other side of the harbor.

"His boat's on the West Dock," Mondrick said. "Hop in. I'll take you over."

Sam followed the harbormaster to a beat-up golf cart.

"I always wanted one of these," he said to Mondrick. "Mind if I drive?"

The harbormaster looked at Sam as he sat down behind the steering wheel, not sure if the cop was being serious or not.

Sam shrugged and walked around to the passenger side. He looked around like an excited kid.

"This is where they filmed Jaws, right?" he asked.

Mondrick let out an audible groan as he maneuvered the golf cart around the harbor to the other dock. While the harbor had been featured in the iconic film, the harbormaster had grown tired of answering questions about the movie - especially since he was just a kid at the time.

"I hope you all finish up soon," Mondrick said as he drove. "I've been lenient with Norm and Vanessa, given the circumstances, but I need that slip. Striped bass season starts next month, and we're cramped for space as it is. I told Vanessa I'd need to move the boat to an outer mooring if I don't get payment by the end of the month."

"And she hasn't paid it yet?" Sam asked.

Dan shook his head. "I think we're both hoping Norm will take care of it when he comes back," he said.

"So you think he's coming back?" Sam asked.

The harbormaster pulled to a stop in front of a blue and white boat backed into a slip between two other similar trawlers and cordoned off with yellow police tape.

"He always does," Mondrick finally answered the question.

20

SAM CLIMBED OUT OF THE GOLF CART AND STARED AT THE 35-foot Deltaga trawler sandwiched between two other trawlers. While in good shape, it was weathered enough for Sam to assume it was an older boat. A large winch and spool at the stern of the boat held thick yellow cable that connected up to a large boom angling out from the center of the boat. Next to the boom, a tall mast jutted straight up, holding several antennas and a radome.

"Mind if I go on board?" Sam asked.

Mondrick shrugged. "If you're working with Paul, then I guess you can go *aboard*," he said, making a point of correcting Sam's language.

Sam didn't seem to notice. Or at least he didn't care. He was just glad the harbormaster hadn't checked with Detective Turner. It was easier if he thought they were working together.

Knowing he was being watched, Sam attempted to hop on to the boat. But there was more space between the dock and the boat's deck than he had counted on and, after a few fumbled attempts, Mondrick shook his head and pulled himself out of the golf cart to help him.

Finally on deck, Sam walked past the mechanicals at the boat's stern and toward the cabin. He opened the cabin door and stepped down into the tiny galley crammed with a small oven and built-in dinette. The boat creaked as it swayed gently and Sam placed a hand on the bulkhead to steady himself as he slowly scooted through a narrow entry into a tiny stateroom with two bunk beds. Sheets were tightly tucked into each thin mattress and sleeping bags were rolled and secured along the back wall. Sam had always thought it would be cool to live on a boat, but there was no way he could last long in this cramped, claustrophobic space. He looked around, noting that every inch of the cabin served a functional purpose. It surprised him at how incredibly neat and orderly everything was. From what he had heard about Norm, he was expecting a sloppy disaster. But he now figured that every part of Norm's life was messy *except* his boat. He took good care of his rig. This was his sanctuary. And, while he knew jack shit about boating, Sam knew it was important to always know where everything was.

"You doing okay in there?" Mondrick called out from the dock.

"When was the last time Norm was out here?" Sam yelled back.

"Can't say for sure," Mondrick answered. "I haven't seen him for over a week."

Sam stepped past the berths to a forward compartment with a large windshield that looked out over the bow of the boat. A chart of New England's coastal waters was taped down on the table with several red X marks and circles on it.

"*Buried treasure*," Sam joked to himself, although he really speculated that they were good fishing spots.

Again, everything was in perfect order. Nothing suspicious. No disarray. It certainly didn't look like the boat of a person planning an ocean getaway.

Sam opened the drawers of the adjacent desk. One of them

held paper supplies, computer cords and other small items. *His junk drawer*, Sam thought to himself.

He slid open another drawer and found a bottle of whiskey and a framed photo of Vanessa. He tried to open a third drawer, but it was locked. He was trying to jimmy the lock when he heard another man approach the dock.

"Hey, he can't be in there," the man said.

Sam crept slowly and silently to the stern of the cabin so he could get a look out the galley window. It was one of the uniformed Chilmark police officers Sam had seen at the police station. Sam grew still, hoping the officer wouldn't notice him, but the cop knelt down and looked through the window directly at Sam.

"Sir, this is a crime scene," the officer said with a practiced, authoritative tone. "I'm going to have to ask you to step off the boat."

"He said he was working with you guys," Mondrick said.

Sam sighed and stepped back out on the deck.

"Just giving it a fresh set of eyes," he said to both men.

"You lied to me," Mondrick yelled.

"I didn't technically lie," Sam replied. "I am working with them. Just not necessarily with their blessing."

Before he could defend himself further, the officer's radio interrupted them. Sam recognized Turner's voice on the other end. Realizing that he had an eavesdropper, the officer stepped away and spoke quietly into his radio. He turned back and looked at Sam nervously. From the look on his face, Sam could tell it was something big.

"What is it, kid?" Sam asked.

The officer ignored him and directed his attention to Mondrick.

"I have to go," he said urgently, turning to Sam. "Off the boat. Now."

Sam watched helplessly as the officer started running

toward his parked patrol car. He turned to face a very red-faced Mondrick.

"Don't suppose you can give me a ride back," he said sheepishly.

Mondrick answered by turning the golf cart around and driving away.

"If you don't want me on the boat, then don't leave me stranded here," Sam yelled as Mondrick drove out of sight.

He slung one foot clumsily over the gunwale of the boat, barely reaching the dock with it. He pushed himself forward and toppled to the dock. He scrambled to his feet, trying to quickly shake off his ungracefulness, and started walking fast around the harbor and back to his truck...and the police scanner.

Had they found Norm? Made some other discovery?

Something was clearly going on, and Sam needed to know.

21

THE WINDING SINGLE-LANE ROAD WAS ALREADY LINED WITH police cars when Sam pulled up. He had been able to put together the general location from what he heard on the police scanner Jude had loaned him. And luckily, Chappaquiddick only had a few main roads, so it helped him narrow down the search. He just drove slowly and waited for a police car to pass him, then followed it.

It had taken him longer than expected to get there. First, he had to drive across the main island from Menemsha to Edgartown. Then he had to figure out how to maneuver all those pesky one-way streets in Edgartown before waiting for the small ferry to cross the harbor between Edgartown and Chappaquiddick.

Even though Sam was growing impatient by the time he got on the small ferry, he couldn't help but be seduced by it. First off, he recognized it immediately from the movie Jaws. That made two Jaws locations in one day. Secondly, he was entranced by the incredible views.

The Chappy Ferry was an old, flat barge that could only carry a handful of cars at a time. It only took a few minutes for it to travel the 527 feet between landings, but during that time, everything seemed to stand still. The occasional squawk of seagulls punctuated the steady chug of the ferry's motor as it churned past the moored sailboats and fishing boats. Sam looked to his left and saw the Edgartown lighthouse guarding the entrance to the harbor in a scene right off a postcard. For a moment, Sam almost forgot he was making a mad dash to a crime scene.

Even though it was literally just a stone's throw across the harbor, Chappaquiddick was vastly different from the bustling town of Edgartown. Except for an occasional house buried deep off the road, there was little sign of life. As he continued to drive inland, the rolling hills and tall pine trees instantly engulfed him and he felt right at home.

The police car he was following pulled over next to all the other police cars and Sam followed suit. He stepped out of the truck and walked down a sandy road to where all the officers seemed to have gathered. Knowing he was about to walk into the lion's den, Sam took a deep breath to prepare himself. He knew his presence would not be welcome, but he needed to see for himself what they had found.

22

KNOWING HE ONLY HAD A FEW MOMENTS BEFORE TURNER SAW him, Sam beelined it toward the first uniformed cop he could find. He did the quick flash of his badge and started talking fast to keep the cop confused and more willing to cooperate.

"Detective Lawson, QPD, helping out with the case," he said matter-of-factly. "I got here as fast as I could. Is that the suspect's car over there? I'm assuming there's no body. Have you started searching the parameter?"

The bombardment of questions seemed to do the trick, and the officer nodded.

"Yes, sir," he said. "That's the suspect's vehicle. And no body has been found."

Sam started walking closer to the maroon Ford Focus, motioning the officer to walk with him. This would keep the officer active and occupied so he wouldn't have time to question Sam's presence. Plus, Sam used the officer as cover from the cluster of cops studying the car.

"Tell me what you've found so far," Sam said.

As he walked, he spotted Turner talking to the uniformed officers. Sam lowered his head, hoping to stay hidden.

"Not much," the officer said. "A hiker spotted the vehicle and called it in. It looks abandoned. Doors were locked, but no keys."

"And no body?" Sam asked.

"What the hell are you doing here?" Turner yelled as he stormed toward Sam.

"Thanks for your help," Sam said to the officer, patting him on the shoulder and turning to face the music as Turner approached.

"Hey, Paul. Small world, huh?" Sam said nonchalantly.

"This is a crime scene and you are way out of your jurisdiction," Turner snapped. "How did you even know about this?"

"I was just driving around, exploring the island," Sam said innocently. "Well, truth be told, I was looking for that bridge. You know, the Kennedy one? Anyway, I wound up getting lost on all these back roads. But then I saw all the police cars and figured someone could offer directions. Is that Norm's car?"

He walked toward it, but Turner stood in front of him to stop him.

"You think I'm that stupid?" he said.

"To know if that's Norm's car?" Sam asked, faking confusion.

"I'm going to have to ask you to leave, Detective Lawson," Turner said as politely as possible.

Sam waved him off.

"Please. Call me Sam," he said. "I'm just a concerned citizen. That is his car, isn't it?"

"Do you want me to arrest you?" Turner asked. "Is that what you want? Because I can do it."

Sam held up his hands in front of him.

"As much as I like a cop that takes requests, I don't want to put you out," Sam said.

"Then leave," Turner said through gritted teeth.

Seeing his attempt at charm wasn't working, Sam let out a sigh and tried a more sincere approach.

"Look, I just want to help out," he said. "I'm not good at vacations. I'm bored. Give me something to do. Anything."

"Well, maybe you should go back to Texas," Turner countered.

Sam shook his head. "You know how it is. It's expensive to change flights, especially on a cop's salary."

"Then go work on Vanessa's lavender farm or something," Turner said. "Just stay away from this investigation."

Sam held his hands out, palms up.

"Do these look like farmer's hands?" he asked. "Come on. I'm a cop. It's what I do. And you've gotta be shorthanded. Let me help."

Sam could tell Turner was thinking about it. He decided to seize the moment.

"You think Norm abandoned his car and is hiding somewhere in the woods?" he asked.

Turner hesitated, then finally gave in.

"He must have figured we'd already been looking for his car since he went missing a week ago. We would have known if he took it on the Steamship Authority ferry back to the mainland," he said. "Chances are he dropped his car here and hiked back to the Chappy ferry. Then he either hopped the big ferry back to the mainland or hitched a boat ride with one of his fishing buddies."

"Let me ask around for you," Sam said. "Talk to the fishermen. Anyone with a boat."

Turner laughed. "If one of them knowingly harbored a fugitive, they're certainly not going to tell a stranger," he said. "Especially one wearing cowboy boots."

"What about video footage?" Sam asked. "Security footage at the harbor. The big ferries. I could look through the footage for you. Free up you and your men."

Turner shook his head and patted Sam on the shoulder.

"We've got it under control, Sam," he said. "I appreciate the offer, but you can help the most by letting us do our job, okay?"

Sam nodded. He was slightly disappointed that Turner hadn't accepted his offer, but was actually relieved he wouldn't have to scour through hours of video footage. Besides, he now had the information he needed. Norm's car had been abandoned. There was no sign of his body and there didn't appear to be any foul play. That meant that Norm was on the run and Turner was focused on finding him, which would make it easier for Sam to focus on other possible suspects. And he knew the perfect place to start.

23

"THERE HAS TO BE A REASON YOU SAID IT," CARLA PRODDED.

Ever since Vanessa had professed her doubts of Norm's innocence, she had evaded the subject.

"I'm just tired," Vanessa said. "I say all kinds of stupid things I don't mean."

"But there had to have been a reason," Carla said.

The two sisters lay on the grass, staring up at the afternoon sky. The bottle of wine had long since been emptied and the two women had abandoned the deck for the backyard, where they were indulging in one of their favorite childhood pastimes: staring up at the clouds and talking about life.

As kids growing up outside of New Orleans, they spent most of their summer days outside - regardless of how hot and humid it would get. The only respite was the large weeping willow tree that grew in an empty field not far from their house. Carla and Vanessa would often lie under the tree and look through the long flowing branches at the blue sky beyond it.

Today, there was no willow offering its shade, but it also wasn't hot enough to need it. Instead, they basked in the warmth of the springtime sun shining down on them. Vanessa had been feeling extra chatty, probably a nervous reaction to all the events of the day. Carla was more than content to just listen. She missed her sister, and her workdays were typically spent looking over dead bodies. Hearing a living human's voice was a welcome novelty to her day.

"Remember the wedding?" Vanessa asked, changing the subject. "That was your first time up here, right?"

"I was so pissed we all had to haul ourselves up to Martha's Vineyard," Carla said, resigning herself to the fact her sister wasn't going to address the fact that she had said she doubted Norm's innocence. "I thought you were so uppity."

"Yeah, that's what most people think when they think of the Vineyard," Vanessa said. "And it can be that, for sure."

"Hell, parts of East Texas can be like that," Carla said. "Although, probably not as preppy."

The two women laughed.

"I was so in love," Vanessa reminisced. "I mean, I still am. But it was so young and new."

"And we were so young and naïve," Carla added.

"Norm's a dreamer," Vanessa went on. "It's what I loved about him from day one. But he's hit so many dead ends. I honestly don't know how he keeps going on."

"Well, he's got you supporting him," Carla said. "That can't hurt."

"He hates that," Vanessa said. "His manly pride. I can't tell you how many times I've had to practically force him to not give up."

"That's mighty big of you," Carla said, immediately realizing it unintentionally sounded sarcastic.

"It's his dream," Vanessa clipped. "And that's all that matters."

Carla sat up.

"But look at you now," she said. "The two of you fight all the time. He disappears on you days at a time, leaving you a wreck. You even wonder if he could have killed someone."

Vanessa recoiled at the words but then mulled them around in her mind.

"I just don't know if I know him anymore," she said. "It's that whole boiling frog thing."

"The way to boil a frog is to slowly turn the heat up so he doesn't even notice?" Carla asked.

"Yeah," Vanessa said.

"You know that's not true, right?" Carla asked. "The frog jumps out of the water when things start heating up."

"Well, you're a buzzkill," Vanessa said with a sly smile. "And that frog has no commitment."

"He is quick to leap to conclusions," Carla said, giggling.

Vanessa let out a laugh so hard, she snorted.

"I find this conversation ribbeting," she said between laughs.

Both women were laughing harder than a few bad puns warranted. A week of pent up sorrow and worry had clearly taken its toll. Vanessa propped herself up on her elbows.

"I don't know what I'd do if you weren't here right now," she said, suddenly serious.

Carla rolled on her side and looked up at her sister. Then she noticed something on her arm.

"What's that?" she said, leaning up.

Vanessa quickly pulled her sleeve down.

"What? Oh, nothing," she said.

Carla sat up.

"Let me see your arm," she said.

"No, it's nothing," Vanessa protested.

But Carla grabbed her sister's arm and yanked up the sleeve to reveal the bandage that was now slightly blood-soaked.

"What the hell?"

24

THE DIVE IN LOOKED VERY DIFFERENT BY THE LIGHT OF DAY, BUT Sam had been expecting that. He had spent enough time in bars to know that they had a Jekyll and Hyde quality about them. Sunlight seemed to expose all the bar's illusions. It pulled back the curtain and exposed the wizard. A bar could address this universal reality one of two ways: they could darken everything to maintain the illusion of night, or they could sweep all the decadence into the corners and put up a false appearance of respectability. That seemed to be the route The Dive In took. A smart move for a bar in a tourist town.

Classic rock was playing quietly on the jukebox, and the sound of yelling and laughing had been replaced by the occasional clinks of plates and glasses. There were only a few patrons: a young couple sharing a plate of fries and two old men sitting separately at the bar. Sam was pretty sure they had been there last night. For all he knew, they never left.

The place had a clean shine about it that gave it more of a wholesome family restaurant vibe instead of the rowdy late-night tavern he had visited the night before. Sam was impressed. Most places couldn't pull off such a dramatic shift to their facade.

He saddled up to the bar at a respectable distance from the other men and looked around for a bartender. He was surprised to spot Cici wiping down a table in the back.

"I'll be right with you," she yelled toward Sam without looking up.

Sam watched as she walked back toward the bar. Most bartenders at late-night taverns were like vampires - pouring drinks all night then sleeping all day. But Cici seemed put together and rested. The only thing that supported his vampire theory was her porcelain white skin.

She smiled in recognition at Sam as she rounded the corner of the bar.

"Tex! You came back for more!"

Sam smiled and nodded. "Can't keep a good man down," he said.

Without asking, Cici poured him a glass of the same beer he had been drinking the night before.

"This one is on me," she said. "Sounds like you've had quite the visit so far."

Sam laughed and nodded, toasting the glass to the bartender before taking a sip. "In light of the circumstances, I don't dare complain," he replied.

"I can't believe it's even real," Cici said. "Especially something so violent. It's fucked up."

"Did you know her?" Sam asked.

Cici shrugged and nodded.

"We weren't gal pals or anything," she said. "But, yeah. She came in from time to time."

"What do you know about her boyfriend?" Sam asked, not wasting time for small talk.

"John?" Cici asked with a shrug. "He's okay. Not much of a

talker. One of those guys that's always pissed at the world for something or other."

"Is he violent?"

Cici laughed. "He's an angry drunk, I can tell you that much," she said. "But a lot of people are. If you're asking if I think he could have killed her, I don't think so. I mean, I saw him and Jane arguing all the time. But that's just the kind of relationship they had, you know? I will say, he was always the one with the olive branch in the end."

Sam nodded. But he knew that didn't prove John's innocence. He knew all too well that many times, it was the peacekeepers that eventually snapped. They would just bottle everything in until it burst out in a violent rage.

"What about Norm?" Cici asked. "I heard the police were looking for him."

Sam was surprised how much Cici knew, and she must have noticed the look of surprise on his face.

"Big bar. Small island," she said with a smirk.

Sam laughed and took another gulp of beer.

"So what's a rock star like you doing at a bar like this?" he asked.

Cici smiled with a wink as if to congratulate him for figuring out her other identity.

"I had to get out of that shit show," she said. "So I moved back here. It's where I grew up. Got a job at the bar and haven't looked back since."

"You don't miss it?" Sam asked.

She grinned.

"There's nothing to miss," she said. "I get to live the best parts of it every night."

Sam nodded and toasted his beer to her.

"Well, I was a big fan then and a bigger fan now," he said.

"And you are my favorite detective from Texas," she replied.

One of the men sitting at the other end of the bar called out for a refill and Cici excused herself, leaving Sam's thoughts to return to the case.

Why did he feel like Norm was innocent? Was it out of allegiance to Carla and Vanessa? Or was it that he was always suspicious of things that seemed obvious?

Cici returned, and Sam was ready with a question.

"So what's your take on Norm?" he asked.

Cici thought about it and shrugged. "I just figure there has to be a reason he's the main suspect. Not like they just pulled his name out of a hat."

Sam nodded. That made sense.

"Also—" she said before stopping herself.

"No," she said, shaking her head. "It's just gossip."

Sam pressed her to tell him, promising to take it with a grain of gossip salt.

"I think Norm was having an affair with Jane," she almost whispered. "But that's just a hunch of my own. I have absolutely no proof and I feel guilty for even saying it out loud."

"I tend to trust a bartender's hunch," Sam said. "What makes you think it?"

Cici pulled up two shot glasses and poured them each a shot of whiskey.

"Norm would come here a lot," she said. "Especially in winter, when fishing was slow. And Jane would come in, too. They would talk and laugh. Sometimes they'd dance. I mean, not slow dancing. Nothing intimate. No PDA or anything. But they were definitely very friendly with each other."

"And you think it was more than just two friends?" Sam pushed.

Cici shrugged.

"I've been bartending a long time," she said. "I know the looks people give each other when they don't think anyone else is watching."

Sam nodded. If anyone could recognize a person's secrets, it would be a bartender. Talk about a student of the human condition. Maybe that's why Sam was always drawn to bars. It was free counseling from an experienced therapist.

"How long had this been going on?" Sam asked.

"I couldn't tell you when it started. I picked up on it a few months ago," Cici said. "But I was still picking up on it right until Norm went missing."

Sam thought about Cici's theory. It did open up several possibilities, but most of them didn't point toward Norm. He knocked back the rest of his beer.

"You know where I can find Mr. Rowe?" he asked.

25

THE SHARP, HIGH-PITCHED RIZZZZZ OF AN AIR WRENCH ECHOED
in the dank and oily mechanic's shop. Sam knocked on the
door, but no one answered, so he let himself into the large
garage.

The hood was up on an old brown Buick and a red pickup
was elevated on a lift, but the mechanical screeches were
coming from a black Lexus convertible.

"Excuse me," Sam yelled over the machine.

Sam saw two legs sticking out from underneath the front of
the car. The mechanic had stopped working, but was making
no attempt at pulling himself out from underneath the
convertible.

"You John Rowe?" Sam asked.

"That depends" a gravelly voice answered from beneath
the car.

"Mind if I ask you a couple of questions?" Sam asked.

"Sorry, man," John answered. "I'm booked solid through the
week."

The loud shriek of the air wrench let Sam know that John
had gone back to work.

"It's about Jane Caplan," Sam yelled.

The air wrench grew silent again. This time, the mechanic wheeled himself out from underneath the car. By the way he looked at Sam, it was clear John wasn't expecting to see a stranger. He stood, grabbing a red rag and wiping the sweat off his forehead.

"You with the police or the press?" John asked. "I don't have anything to say, either way."

"I'm with neither," Sam answered. "Well, sort of. I'm helping the police look into Jane's murder."

"So you're a private detective?" John asked.

Sam nodded, deciding it was easier going along with that explanation. Besides, he kind of liked the sound of it.

"You found that bastard yet?" John asked.

"Which bastard are you talking about?" Sam asked back.

"Norm Mayhew," John said, spitting the words out. "That son of a bitch better pray I don't find him first."

It had only been a day since Jane's body had been found and Sam was surprised to see John back at work instead of home grieving. He was also more angry than sad. But Sam reminded himself that everybody grieved differently. And the first thing a lot of people did was redirect their grief into rage.

"We've got some good leads," Sam lied, hoping it would help disarm John. "Can I ask you about the last time you saw Jane? Did she say anything strange? Act weird? Anything out of the ordinary?"

John shook his head without even trying to recall anything.

"We went to dinner two nights ago, but it was just a normal dinner," John said.

"Did you take her home after?" Sam asked, fishing for anything.

"Yeah. But I just dropped her off," he said. "I had to come back here. My mechanic up and quit on me last week, so I'm balls deep in cars. Which is why I need to get back to work now."

"Did you and Jane have a fight? At dinner?"

The question caught John by surprise.

"What? No," he replied indignantly.

Sam told him that an eyewitness reported seeing the two of them arguing as they left the restaurant. He decided it was best not to tell John *he* was the eyewitness.

John didn't answer right away. He just stared at Sam. Finally, he smiled.

"We had a little disagreement," he said. "I wouldn't call it a fight. Forgot about it before it even ended."

"Can I ask what it was about?" Sam pressed.

"I honestly can't even remember," John answered. "I probably said something stupid, and she took it wrong. You know how those things steamroll."

"She seemed really upset," Sam said.

John studied Sam's face, trying to figure out what he was getting at.

"I may have made a crack about one of her paintings," he said. "Just teasing her about it. You know those abstract paintings. I was teasing her that it looked like a guys'... you know. She overreacted."

Sam nodded, not believing a word of it. John sighed and looked at the ground.

"I apologized in the car and it was water under the bridge by the time I dropped her off," he said.

"And you just dropped her off? Didn't go in or anything? Went right home?" Sam asked.

"Yes. Like I already told the real cops," John said, clearly growing annoyed. "And when I got home, my next-door neighbors were still up and sitting outside. We even talked for a minute. Check it out yourself."

Sam shifted gears back to Norm.

"So I take it you knew Norm Mayhew?" he asked.

"Everyone pretty much knows everyone," John answered. "At least those of us that are here year-round."

"I get it," Sam said. "I live in a small town myself. Everybody knows everybody. And everybody's business."

"I keep to myself," John replied coldly.

"Dating pool is also pretty shallow," Sam continued. "You and Norm ever had to compete for a woman? Maybe for Jane?"

John could tell where Sam was going, but he was too smart to take the bait.

"I knew Norm liked Jane," he offered. "She said he was always calling and showing up unexpected. But she didn't like him. Not that way. I trusted her."

"You ever say anything to him about it?" Sam asked.

"Jane can take care of herself," he snapped back, immediately realizing what he'd said.

"Damnit!" he yelled, slamming a fist into the hood of the convertible.

Sam winced and pointed at the new dent. "Gonna need to add that to your list of repairs."

"I should have walked her inside," John said. "I should have stayed there. Then we'd be burying that asshole instead of..."

He turned away from Sam, unable to finish the sentence.

Sam walked back to the truck, not quite sure what to make of John's performance. Was it real? It seemed a little overdramatic for the strong, silent type. But who was he to judge? Regardless, Sam still had a lot of questions. He looked through the contacts on his phone until he found the name Bobby Lyons. He called the number and was relieved when someone picked up.

"Bobby, hey. It's Sam Lawson. I need you to look up a criminal history for a John Rowe in Chilmark, Massachusetts."

26

THE LARGE SCRATCH ON VANESSA'S ARM HAD SHOCKED CARLA AT first. Her sister had brushed it off, explaining it was from an accident at the lavender farm but nothing to worry about. Carla had inspected the gash and decided it wasn't as bad as it originally looked - not bad enough for stitches, anyway. She cleaned and dressed the cut properly and applied fresh bandages.

Once they had lost their afternoon buzz, they decided they were hungry, so Carla volunteered to run to the general store in Chilmark to pick up some more first aid supplies and sandwiches. The store was well-known for its deli. In fact, more customers came to the store for the food than for store items.

Carla paid for the sandwiches and decided to wait for her food outside, on the large covered porch. She maneuvered her way down the narrow aisle and, as she walked out the door, she bumped into the nurse who claimed to be Jane's best friend. The nurse sheepishly glanced at Carla and apologized quietly before sharing a spark of recognition.

"Didn't I see you at the hospital yesterday?" the nurse asked.

Carla introduced herself and asked if the two could talk.

The women walked outside and sat on one of the patio's wooden benches.

"I'm Gina Moffett," the nurse said, shaking Carla's hand.

Her hand was trembling and Carla could tell she had been crying.

"Sorry," Gina said, pulling her hand back. "I'm still pretty shaken up about everything. You must think I'm a complete basket case after the scene I made at the hospital."

"Well, that asshole did nothing to help the situation," Carla offered.

Gina shrugged. "He was right, though. I should have been paying better attention."

"I heard Detective Turner say Jane was your friend," Carla said. "I can't imagine how hard this must be on you."

Gina nodded and visibly fought being overwhelmed with emotion.

"Did I hear you say you were a medical examiner?" she asked.

The quick change of topic shocked Carla. She told Gina that she was a medical examiner in Texas and was on the island visiting her sister.

"I know Vanessa," Gina said. "She's going through her own hell right now. I should probably call her. Is she okay?"

Carla hid her surprise. According to her sister, she and Gina barely knew each other. But the way Gina was talking, they were more friendly than Vanessa had let on.

Carla told Gina how Vanessa was beside herself with grief that Norm was still missing. But the entire time she was talking, she could tell Gina was not so much listening as waiting for a chance to say something else.

"I don't trust Dr. Vincent," she said, shifting the topic again. "He's not going to do a thorough autopsy. And he's just going to tell Detective Turner whatever he wants to hear."

"I can't imagine he wouldn't have some modicum of profes-
sionalism," Carla said.

Gina laughed. "You clearly don't know Dr. Vincent."

She paused before speaking again.

"It wouldn't be possible for you to—"

Her voice trailed off, so Carla finished for her.

"You want me to take a look?" Carla asked.

"Just to provide a second opinion," Jane said. "Or at the very
least, confirm Dr. Vincent's report."

"I wish I could," Carla said. "But I've got no jurisdiction up
here. I mean, I could operate as an independent auditor, but
only from a court order."

"You're right," Gina sighed.

"However," Carla said, before pausing to think a second
before finishing her thought.

"If I were to maybe 'unofficially' see the autopsy report, I
could maybe point out any flaws."

Gina smiled and immediately looked lighter. Right on cue,
Carla's order number was called out, and she stood to walk
back inside.

"I'll give you my number," Carla said.

Gina stood, too. But instead of walking toward the door, she
gently grabbed Carla's arm.

"There's something else," Gina said.

27

CARLA GRABBED HER SANDWICHES AND CAME BACK OUTSIDE where Gina was waiting, except she had moved to a more secluded picnic table so they could have more privacy.

"Jane told me something recently and made me swear not to tell," Gina said as soon as Carla sat down. "I didn't tell the police, but it's going to come out in the autopsy anyway, so it won't be a secret much longer."

"What is it?" Carla asked.

Gina took a deep breath of courage and exhaled loudly.

"Jane had just found out she was pregnant," Gina said in barely a whisper.

"Like, just found out?" Carla asked.

Gina nodded.

"She only told me yesterday. She hadn't even been to a doctor yet. It was just from a home pregnancy test. Actually, from six of them. She wanted to be sure."

"Her boyfriend...John, right? Did he know?" Carla asked.

Gina seemed to struggle with the answer.

"I'm assuming he was the father," Carla said.

"Probably," Gina finally said. "I mean, more than likely, right?"

"You don't sound so sure," Carla said.

Gina went on to explain that Jane had been kind of weird about it.

"There was something she wasn't telling me," Gina said. "And maybe I'm just reading too much into it. Still, even if John was the father, I know Jane didn't want a baby."

"I'm guessing John didn't either," Carla offered.

"She said she'd tell me more after she talked to someone," Gina said. "I assumed that someone was John."

Carla recalled Sam telling her about seeing them arguing the night of her murder.

"And she didn't say anything else?" Carla asked.

Gina shook her head.

"One reason we were such good friends is we stayed out of each other's business," Gina said. "We kind of had an unofficial 'Don't Ask, Don't Tell' policy."

A thought popped into Carla's head.

"Did Jane know Norm?" she asked.

"Yeah, sure," Gina said with a shrug. "But they hadn't spoken to each other in a while. They had a falling out about something. I'm not sure what."

"Don't Ask, Don't Tell," Carla parroted. "Let me ask you a weird question. Do you think Norm could have been the father?"

The question threw Gina off, and she shook her head at the absurdity of the notion.

"I can't even imagine it," she said.

But then she considered the possibility.

"Oh, my God," she muttered. "It sure would explain a lot, wouldn't it?"

28

SAM PUSHED A FEW THROW PILLOWS ASIDE AS HE SAT DOWN ON Vanessa's overstuffed green couch. Carla handed him her laptop, and he quickly opened it to log in to his work email.

As soon as Carla had left the deli, she had called Sam to tell him about Jane's pregnancy. The two had wanted to meet in private—away from Vanessa—to compare notes. Their plan was to meet up at a coffee shop with Wi-Fi, but when Carla had stopped to drop off her sister's sandwich and pick up her laptop, Vanessa had pleaded for her sister to stay. Feeling guilty, Carla had reluctantly agreed and called Sam back to the house. Still, they knew it would be best if Vanessa wasn't around while they talked about the case. So Sam planned a diversion.

"That was a great idea to call Jude," Carla said, watching Sam slowly and methodically type his password on the laptop's keyboard.

"I had to thank him anyway," Sam said. "That police scanner he loaned me is already worth its weight in gold."

Sam had called Jude and asked if he could distract Vanessa somehow. Luckily, mid-spring was a busy time for their lavender farm and it wasn't hard for Jude to come up with a long list of things he needed to discuss with her. He came over under the pretense of discussing some spreadsheets and they both retreated to her home office. As soon as they had left, Sam sprang into action, grabbing Carla's laptop.

Carla and Sam had already shared everything they had learned, but were no closer to any real answers than they had been at the start of the day. Even the discovery of Norm's car didn't necessarily prove he was alive and on the run. Someone could have stolen the car and recently abandoned it. Everything else they found was nothing more than gossip and speculation.

"So you think John did it?" Carla asked point blank.

"I can't say he didn't do it," Sam answered. "But I do know that our local detective friend has turned a blind eye to his buddy. I'm not ready to do that yet."

After several mistyped attempts, Sam finally logged in to his account. He had received a text from his dispatch in Texas to tell him he had emailed a copy of John Rowe's criminal history. Sam opened the document and Carla moved in close beside him so she could see better. Her hair brushed against Sam's cheek and he closed his eyes to breathe in the familiar scent of her shampoo. If it were up to him, he'd throw the laptop on the floor and turn his full attention to Carla. He'd come all this way just to be with her, and they had spent most of the day apart. But he was smart enough to know that Carla's attention was on helping her sister right now — so that's where he was, too.

"Let's see what our friend John has been up to," Sam muttered, bringing his attention back to the laptop screen.

The two of them read through the laundry list together. It wasn't that extensive. And most of it was at least ten years old. A couple of drunk and disorderlies. A few assaults. All alcohol related.

"What do you make of it?" Carla asked.

"The guy used to drink a lot and get into bar fights," Sam answered.

"Sounds like someone else I know," Carla teased, elbowing Sam in the ribs.

It was true. Sam had a well-earned reputation as a drunk and a troublemaker. Although he considered it a point of pride to Sam that he had never thrown the first punch. It was his smart mouth and not his temper that always got him into trouble. He had a knack for pissing off the wrong person.

If nothing else, Sam was living proof that the kind of arrests on John's record were no indication he could commit murder. Especially one as violently as Jane's attack. On the other hand...

"He's got a temper," Carla said. "Maybe he just snapped. You said they'd been fighting earlier. Maybe she had told him about the pregnancy. He got angry and they fought. Maybe she had decided to keep the baby, and he didn't want to deal with being a father. Or maybe Jane told him he wasn't the father, and he flew off in a jealous rage."

Sam nodded. "All good theories. But they're no more than speculation. I need proof."

Carla needled Sam again. "Since when has Sam Lawson let something like proof stop him?"

Sam chuckled. He did tend to trust his gut more than evidence. But he also knew Turner wouldn't be interested in any theories from him. The only way he was going to get Turner's attention would be with hard proof.

"We need to retrace Jane's steps the other night," Sam thought out loud.

"Phone records?" Carla asked.

"Yeah, that would definitely be helpful," Sam said. "But I'm sure Turner is already on that, and I'm guessing he won't be sharing."

"What if you could get into her phone bill?" Carla asked. "Would it show her calls and texts?"

"Definitely," Sam answered, shutting the laptop in frustration. "But unless you know a hacker..."

Carla pulled out her phone and scrolled through pictures. She let out a happy gasp of surprise and Sam turned to see the mischievous smile on her face.

"You don't need a hacker if you have her password," she said, holding up her phone.

29

SAM SQUINTED AT THE PHOTO CARLA WAS SHOWING HIM ON HER phone.

"What am I looking at here?" he said.

"While we were waiting for the police after finding Jane's body, I took some pictures," Carla explained. "Crime scene photos. Force of habit."

Sam looked at her and smiled. She was sneakier than he thought.

"Look on the fridge," she said, pointing again to the photo on her phone.

She zoomed in and Sam waited for the image to refocus.

"I still don't know what I'm looking at," he said. "Is that a grocery list?"

Carla groaned in exasperation and took the phone back.

"No," she said. "It's a list of her passwords. Bank account. Facebook account...Phone bill."

Sam couldn't believe what Carla was telling him. He took her phone back and looked again at the image. Carla was right. It was a list of about ten of Jane's personal accounts, with the corresponding username and password.

"Holy shit," Sam said in disbelief.

Carla giggled in amusement at Sam's surprise.

"Not the safest way to store your security information," she said. "But I'm not complaining."

"You're brilliant," Sam said.

He took her face in his hands and gave her a big kiss. Handing the phone back to Carla, he opened the laptop again. He googled the cell phone company's website and typed in the login information as Carla read it to him. In an instant, they were in her account.

He searched around on the site until he found a tab that read "Minute Details."

"These must be calls," Sam said as he clicked on the tab.

Sure enough, it opened a call log that went back thirty days. Not only did it show the date and time of all incoming and outgoing calls, but also the number of the other caller.

Carla grabbed a notepad and started jotting down phone calls that happened two nights ago after 8 p.m.

"Looks like there's just a couple," Sam said. "One was for just a few minutes. The other was nine minutes long."

"What about unanswered calls?" Carla asked.

Sam shook his head. That kind of information would be available to Turner and the Chilmark police, but Jane's phone bill didn't go into that kind of detail.

"Does it list texts?" Carla asked.

Sam clicked back and found another tab labelled "Message Details." He clicked it and found another log of numbers. This time there were more entries.

"Looks like she received several texts from one number, but there are no outgoing texts to it," Sam said as Carla scribbled down the number.

There seemed to be an exchange with a second number - the same number as the quick call. Several texts back and forth, shortly after midnight.

Only four other texts from that night, all involving the same number: one outgoing and one incoming text around 7:00 and then the same pattern again at 10:30.

"So it looks like there were only three people she texted with that night," Sam said as he put together a timeline. "And she also spoke to two of those people. Person A called her around 6:00 and they talked for about nine minutes. They also sent ten total texts back and forth just after midnight."

Using *67 to block her number from Caller ID, Carla dialed the number and wasn't surprised to get John Rowe's voicemail.

"That makes sense," Sam said. "John called her, maybe to make plans for their date. Then they texted later on after midnight."

"Probably still arguing from earlier," Carla added.

"Which we can now assume was probably about her being knocked up," Sam said.

"Which also would mean she was still alive when he left her house," Carla added.

Sam nodded reluctantly. He hated when facts blew up his theories.

"This next number sounds familiar," Carla said. "Hang on."

She grabbed her purse and rifled through it until she found the piece of paper Gina had given her earlier with her phone number. She checked it against the phone records.

"So it looks like Jane called Gina around 6:15," Carla said. "Probably telling her she had a date with John and getting a little pep talk because of the bombshell she was going to drop."

"Then Jane texts her when she gets to the restaurant at 7:00," Sam said. "I saw Jane and John arguing around 10:00, so that would mean she could have been home by the time she texted Gina the last time."

"Then there's this third phone number," Carla said.

"There were no calls to or from Person C, but they sent her nine texts between 11:00 and 11:45. p.m."

"And she never replied," Carla said.

"She clearly didn't want to talk to this person."

"Shit," Carla said as she looked down at her phone.

She held up her phone to show Sam what she found. She had entered the third phone number into her phone and it had matched to one of her contacts.

30

CARLA AND SAM HAD DECIDED IT WAS TIME TO INVOLVE VANESSA in their investigation. Maybe she had answers that would clear things up. Armed with Carla's phone and laptop, the couple went back to the office where Vanessa and Jude were working.

Carla told her sister how she and Sam had been using Jane's phone bill to trace her steps from two nights ago and they had come across a familiar number. Sam opened the laptop and showed it to Vanessa. She stared at it in shock, finally shaking her head.

"That can't be right," Vanessa said.

"Sure looks like Norm's number to me," Sam said.

"But why would he call Jane?" Vanessa asked. "Why wouldn't he call me?"

"Were Norm and Jane friends?" Carla asked gently.

Vanessa stood up in a huff and started pacing nervously.

"I just don't understand," she said.

"We've heard some of the rumors," Sam said, ignoring the steely stare Carla threw at him.

"This island loves a good scandal," Vanessa said. "If they can't find one, they'll make one up."

"So you don't think they're true then?" Sam asked. "The rumors about Norm and Jane?"

"I know they aren't true," Vanessa snapped. "Norm swore to me there was nothing going on between them."

"They were at least talking," Sam said, pointing to the laptop screen.

Vanessa glared at Sam, shocked that he could even ask such a question.

"Whose side are you on?" she yelled before storming out of the room.

Carla got up to follow her sister, but not before hissing at Sam.

"Could you try to be a little sensitive? Just pretend," she said.

Sam was surprised they both had turned on him so quick. He looked up at Jude, who was also glaring at him. He started to say something in his defense, but Jude shook his head.

"Tread lightly, son," he said.

Sam heard a door slam and then Carla knocking on it, asking Vanessa to open it.

Maybe he had been a little rough. But he was asking the questions that any detective would have asked. He knew that most wives, when confronted with evidence that their husband was having an affair, were already suspicious. And he could tell that Vanessa was a little too defensive about the whole thing. Either she was in a severe state of denial or she was hiding something. Either way, Sam had a feeling that something just didn't seem right.

Carla came back in the room, her face red with anger.

"Well, she's locked herself in her room," she said. "Good job, Sam."

"I never accused Norm of anything," Sam said.

"You might as well have," Carla said. "It's bad enough her

husband is missing and wanted for murder. Now you're going to throw an affair on top of it?"

"Why else would he be calling another woman in the middle of the night?" he asked. "To get a cake recipe?"

Unable to come up with a suitable answer, Carla sat down beside Sam with a groan.

"Vanessa is fragile," Jude said. "You best tread lightly."

"How much do you know about her marriage?" Sam asked. "Other than the occasional fight?"

Jude clenched his jaw and walked past Sam, stopping to stare him directly in the eyes.

"You're talking about my son and my daughter-in-law," he growled. "I won't be a part of this."

He stormed out of the room, leaving a befuddled Sam to turn to Carla.

"How much do you know?" he asked her.

"I know they love each other," she answered softly. "Sometimes they just have a hard time living with each other."

Her calm tone helped ease the tension in the room. Sam sat next to Carla.

"Do you think he'd ever cheat on her?" Sam asked.

Carla shook her head.

"I don't think so."

"Had Vanessa ever even suspected it?"

"Probably," Carla answered. "Everyone does at some point or another, right?"

Sam thought about it. Carla was the first serious relationship he'd had in over a decade, but he couldn't even imagine her cheating on him. It wasn't in her nature. Still, when she had wanted to take a break for a little while, Sam had become incredibly jealous and paranoid. If she even spoke to a man, he worried that she was dating him. A bolt of pain and adrenaline would shoot through him at the mere thought of her with another man. If he were to allow himself to get lost in his paranoia, he'd turn into a tumbling mass of rage, pain and insecurity. Even just thinking about it was stirring up those emotions, and he felt embarrassed for feeling so vulnerable.

Embarrassed.

"If your sister found out Norm was having an affair, are you sure she would tell you?" he asked.

"I would think so," she said.

"Maybe she'd be too embarrassed to say anything," Sam continued. "That'd be a tough thing to admit to your little sister. Especially if she felt responsible."

"Why would she feel responsible if he cheated?" Carla asked.

Sam shrugged. "Stuff like that brings out people's insecurities."

"No," Carla said. "She'd tell me."

"But what if—and I'm being purely hypothetical—what if what you know about Vanessa is only what she wants you to know?" Sam asked.

"What are you getting at, Sam?" Carla asked defensively.

"I'm just thinking out loud."

Carla jumped up. "You think she's hiding something from me?"

Before Sam could answer, they were interrupted by a knock at the front door.

31

Carla tried to hide her surprise when she opened the door to Detective Turner.

"Hello, Miss Davenport," Turner said. "Is your sister here?"

Turner followed Carla where Jude and Sam were waiting. He deflated with a loud sigh when he saw the detective.

"Paul! How the hell you been?" Sam said in an exaggerated friendliness.

"Lawson," Turner said, making no effort to hide his disdain.

He nodded at Jude who answered back with his own nod.

"I'm here to see Vanessa," Turner said. "Just Vanessa."

"They can stay," Vanessa said, her voice surprising both men.

Vanessa had emerged from her bedroom. Her eyes were puffy and bloodshot. It was obvious she'd been crying.

"Have you found him?" she asked, almost afraid of any answer he could offer.

"Yes and no," Turner said.

"Oh, God," Vanessa said.

Carla helped her sit down and Jude walked over by her side.

"This ain't a good time to be cagey, Paul," Sam said.

"It's detective. Detective Turner," Turner replied. "And I wasn't trying to be cagey."

He turned his attention back to Vanessa, glancing up at Jude.

"Security footage spotted Norm getting off the ferry at Woods Hole around 11:00 a.m. yesterday morning," Turner said.

Vanessa let out a sigh of relief.

"But now he's gone again?" Jude asked with a slight tremble in his voice.

"Did he get in a car? Catch a cab?" Sam asked.

Turner shook his head. "We only caught him on the dock camera," he said. "There was no sign of him on the south lot camera, and the north lot camera...wasn't working."

"But he's alive," Vanessa said.

Turner nodded.

"It would appear so," he said. "But it also means he was most likely on the island at the time of the murder. We've issued an APB for all of Massachusetts."

"And there was no other sign of him?" Sam asked.

"If there were, I'd be there instead of here," Turner answered, clearly annoyed. "Vanessa, I know I've asked you before, but it's really important...do you have any idea where he might be?"

Vanessa shook her head as she began to sob.

"If she did, don't you think she would have already told you that?" Carla asked. "We've been looking for him for a week now."

Turner nodded. "I know. I'm sorry. I was just grasping at straws. If you think of anything, please let me know."

"Is there any way I can help?" Sam asked.

Turner stood to face Sam, the compassion on his face immediately hardening into contempt. He motioned for Sam to follow him out of earshot of the others.

"I understand you already took it upon yourself to talk to

John," he said quietly. "I'm getting tired of saying this but I'd appreciate it if you would step back and let me do my job."

Sam nodded and glanced at Carla to let her know this probably wasn't the best time to bring up their phone discoveries. Besides, it was nothing that Turner wouldn't find out on his own.

"Stay away from John," Turner said again, making his point clear.

"I'm driving Norm's old work truck. What if it breaks down?" Sam asked. "Can I call him then? I promise to keep the conversation completely vehicular."

Sam noticed Turner clench his jaw and that made him smile. He showed the detective to the door and watched him drive away, then he turned to Vanessa.

"Did Norm keep all of his stuff in the office?" he asked.

Vanessa nodded. "But we've already been through everything. There's nothing there."

"Where else would Norm keep things?" Sam asked.

"His boat," Jude answered. "But the cops aren't letting anyone near it."

Sam paced the room, thinking. A smile spread across his face as a plan began to hatch. He looked at Jude and grinned mischievously.

"Want to have a little fun?"

32

Jude turned his headlights off as he pulled to the side of the road. Sam sat in the passenger seat and looked out over Menemsha Harbor.

"You sure you're okay with this?" Sam asked him.

"If this will help find my son," Jude answered. "Then I'll do what I have to do."

They both got out of the car and walked down the street to the harbor. The sun had set only an hour earlier, but the harbor was already growing dark and a light fog had drifted in from the Sound. Faint lights from the windows of a few boats glowed through the mist, hinting at some signs of life, but most of the vessels were blackened silhouettes sleeping on the water.

As the two men reached the harbor parking lot, they crouched behind a parked truck to assess the situation. They spotted someone on the West Dock, near Norm's boat. He was looking at his phone and there was just enough glow from the screen for Sam and Jude to tell he was wearing a police uniform.

"There's your man," Sam said, handing Jude a bottle of whiskey.

Jude screwed off the lid and poured some out.

"What are you doing?" Sam whispered excitedly.

"I can't very well be drunk if I have a full bottle," Jude answered matter-of-factly.

He stood and started stumbling toward the harbor, humming loudly. Sam waited until Jude had reached the docks, then he began creeping through the shadows in the same direction.

"Jimmy? Is that you?" Jude yelled at the officer.

"Mr. Mayhew?" the officer asked, squinting toward the man walking toward him. "What are you doing here?"

Jude got closer, putting his hand on the officer's shoulder.

"You hear about my boy?" Jude asked, purposefully slurring his words.

The officer took an uncomfortable step back. "I did, sir," he said. "This has to be pretty rough on you."

Jude raised the bottle of whiskey and grinned. "We all have our trials and tribulations."

"What are you doing here?" the officer asked again.

Jude walked past the officer, forcing the officer to turn away from the dock entrance.

"I was hoping I could get some things off his boat," Jude said, pointing at Norm's boat behind him.

"I'm sorry, sir. I can't let you on there," the officer explained. "Police order."

Jude looked over the officer's shoulder to see Sam moving toward them through the shadows. He nodded to the officer.

"I understand," he slurred. "But maybe just for a second?"

"Come on, Mr. Mayhew," the officer said. "Let's get you back home."

He started to turn around toward the dock entrance...and Sam.

"I'm just gonna go on the boat," Jude said loudly to distract the officer.

The cop spun back around to stop Jude. It was just enough time for Sam to scramble on another boat and hide out of sight. Once Jude was satisfied Sam was hidden, he laughed.

"I'm just kidding," he said. "I am a law-abiding citizen and respect you and that uniform."

He saluted at the cop.

"Thank you, Mr. Mayhew," the flustered cop said. "Can I help get you home?"

"Just point me in the right direction," he slurred, looking around.

Sam peered over the side of the boat he was hiding in, marveling at Jude's drunk performance. Who knew this stoic man had such a flare for drama?

A star is born, Sam thought.

Jude started walking in the wrong direction, veering close to the edge and pretending to almost lose his balance.

"Let me help you," the officer said, as he put his hand on Jude's shoulder to steady him.

"I just need to get to my car," Jude said.

"I don't think you should be driving, sir" the officer said as he guided Jude back down the pier.

"I'll get in back and sleep it off," Jude slurred. "It's a wonderful night to sleep under the stars."

Sam hunched down as the two men passed him. He finally sat up to make sure Jude was leading the officer further away. Once he felt the cop was far enough, he slowly crawled back on to the dock and crept to Norm's boat.

33

SAM INCHED CAREFULLY THROUGH THE BOAT'S CABIN, TRYING NOT to make any noise or create any movement, while also attempting to maneuver in the dark. With his hands in front of him, he felt his way along the bulkheads, through the galley and then the stateroom. Finally, he made it to the navigation station. The large front windshield let in just enough moonlight for Sam to see.

Jude's performance was still keeping the officer occupied. Sam could hear him singing loudly from what was probably the parking lot and was pretty impressed at his drunk act. He clearly knew his way around the bottle. It wasn't over the top and obnoxious. Just "off" enough to be believable without being annoying.

The loud singing had been Sam's idea to gauge how far away the officer was from the boat. Knowing they were in the parking lot - and probably just out of sight - Sam dropped to his knees and turned his attention to the locked third drawer. He pulled a lock pick set from his pocket and slid the long, thin pick into the drawer's opening. He smiled, happy he had thrown the small kit into his duffel before his trip. Admittedly, he had done it out of blind habit, but he preferred to think of it as instinctive foresight.

He inserted the pin into the keyhole and gently jiggled it until he heard the soft click of the pins setting. Sam smiled and pulled the drawer open slowly, peering inside. There was a box of envelopes, some spare lightbulbs and a loose pile of paper. Sam slid the papers out from underneath the other objects and set them on the floor in front of him. He cupped his hand over the front of a small flashlight and turned it on. His hand dimmed the light perfectly, and Sam could spread his fingers ever so slightly to cast just enough of a glow to read.

There was a rental agreement for the dock slip, a couple of parking tickets and some old bank statements. There was also an envelope that contained some sort of contract. Sam began reading it and realized it was an informal lease agreement.

Sam suddenly became aware that Jude had stopped singing. He rose and peered out the cabin window toward the parking lot. He couldn't see anyone heading back to the dock, but Jude had stopped singing, which was the code that he needed to hurry things up. He was just about to scoop up the papers when a boisterous laugh broke the night's silence. While Jude's laugh was loudest, Sam could make out a second laugh.

Good, he thought. *The cop is still with him.*

He dropped back to his knees to take a closer look at the lease agreement. It seemed to be for a mobile home in a trailer park. Sam skimmed the document for an address and finally found it. The trailer park was in Dennis, Massachusetts.

Remembering there was a chart at the nav station, Sam stood up slowly to take a look. It took him awhile, but he finally found what he was looking for. If Cape Cod was an arm flexed to make a muscle, Boston would be the shoulder, Chatham would be the elbow and Provincetown would be the fist. Dennis would be the bicep.

"Oh, come on!" Jude's voice yelled from the parking lot. "You don't have to go back yet, do you?"

Sam looked out the window again. He could see the silhouette of Jude at the edge of the parking lot, yelling toward the silhouette of the officer, who was walking back in his direction. Sam's heart began to race. Once the cop reached the dock, there would be no way Sam could get past him without being seen. He'd be trapped. Suddenly, Jude let out a strange yell and fell to the ground. The cop turned and ran back over to the fallen fake drunk. Knowing he didn't have much time, Sam scooped up the rental lease and fumbled his way through the dark cabin and off the boat.

34

"I HAVE NO IDEA WHAT THIS IS," VANESSA SAID.

She was sitting on the couch, staring in disbelief at the rental agreement Sam had laid out in front of her.

"Y'all never rented a trailer home in Dennis?" Sam asked again.

Vanessa looked past Sam to Carla and Jude, who were looking on with concern.

"Why would he rent a trailer home and not tell me?" Vanessa asked.

"Well, at least you probably know where he runs off to," Sam said.

Vanessa's confusion was shifting to anger.

"I bet he's got some tramp living there," she seethed.

Carla knelt in front Vanessa.

"Don't jump to any conclusions," she said. "The lease was signed two years ago."

"But there's no termination date," Jude chimed in.

Carla shot a glare at Jude to let him know he wasn't helping.

"We need to turn this over to Paul," Sam said. "The cops'll check it out."

"No!" Vanessa exclaimed.

She stood and clutched Sam's hands in hers.

"You need to check it out first," she said.

"What?" Sam asked. "That borders on obstruction. I like you, Vanessa, but I'm not going to jail for you."

"Detective Turner has it out for Norm," Vanessa pleaded. "I'd be afraid of what would happen if he found him first."

"Paul's not gonna hurt him," Sam argued.

"You don't know that," Vanessa said. "He thinks Norm is armed and dangerous. One false move and they'd start shooting."

"Maybe she's right," Jude interrupted. "I don't trust my son if he's cornered by the police. But if you found him, you could bring him in. Peacefully."

"Why don't you go get him?" Sam asked.

Jude shook his head. "He probably would react worse to seeing me than he would the cops."

Sam took a step back and started pacing.

"Jesus, what is it with you people?" he asked.

"May I remind everyone that we don't even know if he's there," Carla said. "It's a long shot, at best. And if we send the police on that wild goose chase that's less time they can look for the actual killer."

Sam looked at Carla as if she had betrayed him.

"You too, Bluto?"

Carla smiled and shook her head.

"It's 'Et tu, Brutus,' " she said.

"That doesn't even make sense," Sam argued.

"You're getting off track," Vanessa interrupted.

Sam looked at Carla. Hers was the only voice he trusted, and he had to admit she made a good point. The chance of Norm being there was a long shot. If he told Turner and it led to a dead end, all it would have done was piss Turner off and, more importantly, pull him and his team away from the investigation. And if Norm *was* there, but he was as reactive as Vanessa and Jude said, there was a good chance that things could go south quickly if the cops cornered him. Sam wouldn't say it to the others, but he also worried about a cop planting evidence to speed things along.

Sam let out a groan as he nodded his head.

"I'm coming with you," Jude said.

Sam turned to Jude with a smirk.

"Got a taste for it, huh?" Sam teased. "This detective work is fun, right?"

Jude did not smile back.

"He's my son," he replied firmly.

35

CARLA POURED SOME MORE PINOT NOIR INTO VANESSA'S WINE glass and watched as her sister raised it to her lips with a trembling hand.

"Chances are he's not going to be there," Carla said, realizing that was only somewhat comforting.

Vanessa shook her head. "I can't decide if I'm scared or pissed," she said. "What kind of double life was he living?"

Carla sat down next to her sister. "It may be nothing," she said. "It could have been an old, expired lease."

"He still rented it," Vanessa said. "And never told me about it."

Carla struggled for how to put the question that had been on her mind all day.

"Did you and Norm fight a lot?" she finally asked. "I mean... like this?"

"Never like this," Vanessa said. "We've had some nasty ones, but he never ran off for more than a day."

Vanessa emptied her glass of wine and motioned for Carla to hand her the bottle. Carla gathered the courage to ask the real question she had.

"Did he ever...cheat on you?" Carla asked gently.

Carla noticed her sister pause for a second before pouring her wine.

"I don't know," she said weakly. "I really don't."

"Oh, Nessie. That's horrible. I'm so sorry," Carla said. "Why didn't you tell me?"

Vanessa laughed. "Because I'm the older sister," she said. "I'm supposed to have my shit together. You're the baby. You're supposed to look up to me. But you've always had to take care of me. Pick me back up. Do you know how hard it is to have such a fucked-up life and then look at your baby sister and see how put together she is? It's embarrassing."

It was Carla's turn to laugh.

"You think I'm put together?" she asked. "Oh, Honey. You have no idea. I'm a hot mess."

She started listing her faults.

"I'm a control freak," she said. "I close myself off emotionally. I'm in my forties and barely had a serious relationship. At least one long enough to matter."

"You left me with mom and dad to go off to college," Vanessa added.

That one caught Carla off guard.

"You talked me into going," Carla said. "I didn't want to. Remember?"

Vanessa nodded, admitting that Carla was right.

"I was just trying to be the noble, selfless big sister for once," she said. "I didn't think you'd actually go through with it."

Carla laughed.

"What else?" Vanessa said. "How else are you a mess? I'm enjoying this."

Carla smiled and thought about it.

"I nearly threw Sam away because it got a little uncomfortable," she said. "My dreaded fear of the unknown."

"Thank God you came to your senses on that one," Vanessa said. "Sam's a little rough around the edges at times, but he's a good man."

"He is," Carla replied. "I just felt like I needed to have all my shit together before I could handle a relationship."

"Sometimes it's the relationship that helps you get your shit together," Vanessa said before raising her glass in a toast. "And sometimes, the relationship creates more shit of its own."

Carla clinked her glass to her sister's. "Here's to the shit."

The two sisters laughed and continued talking until Vanessa finally excused herself to go to bed. It was while Carla was putting the wine glasses in the sink that she noticed she had a text message from a number she didn't recognize. She opened the phone screen and was surprised at what she read:

MEET ME AT THE DIVE IN AT 11 P.M. COME ALONE.

36

Sᴀᴍ sɴᴜᴄᴋ ᴀʀᴏᴜɴᴅ ᴛᴏ ᴛʜᴇ ʙᴀᴄᴋ ᴏғ ᴛʜᴇ ᴍᴏʙɪʟᴇ ʜᴏᴍᴇ. Tʜᴇʀᴇ were no lights on and it looked uninhabited, but Sam had had some bad experiences with mobile homes and he knew better to make any assumptions.

Jude had parked his truck up the road and out of sight, and Sam had walked from there. It not only gave Sam the element of surprise, but it allowed Jude to act as a lookout if someone took off running.

Sam crouched below a window, then slowly stood up to peer inside. Even though it was dark, it was a clear night, and the moon was almost full—enough to cast its pale blue glow over the weed-infested back yard, creating a reflection on the window that made it hard to see inside.

Sam cupped his hands to shield out the reflection, but it was too dark inside. Still, he crept around the outside of the mobile home, checking the full perimeter. Finally, he circled back around to the front door. He pulled the screen door open slowly. Thankfully, it wasn't creaky. He slowly twisted the door-knob and wasn't surprised to find it locked. Luckily, it was a fairly simple door knob with no dead bolt. Sam could pick those kinds of locks in his sleep.

Sam pulled the small lock pick set from his pocket, once again congratulating himself on his own resourcefulness. He slid a pick and small tensioner wrench out of a sleeve and knelt by the lock, using the tools to carefully release the lock's inner pins. In less than a minute, the doorknob turned freely. Sam stood, put the lock pick set away and pulled out his handgun.

He pushed the door open with one hand, the other holding the pistol at the ready. With the moonlight at his back, he knew he was a sitting duck of a silhouette so he quickly stepped out of the door path and into the shadows. The open door allowed some moonlight inside, and Sam stood still as he let his eyes adjust.

The door had opened into the living room, which was completely empty and looked like it had been for a long time. Sam began to think he had barked up the wrong tree, but wasn't yet ready to let his guard down. He looked to his right and could make out another room. There was also a hallway to his left. If this mobile home followed the layout of other mobile homes, the room to his right would be an eat-in kitchen and the hallway to his left would lead to a couple of bedrooms and a bath.

Sam started with the kitchen. If there would be any sign of life, that's where it would be.

He snaked along the wall, walking lightly to stay as quiet as possible. Sure enough, the room was a small kitchen. And it appeared to have been recently occupied. A small folding table, covered with beer cans and pizza boxes, sat in the middle of the room. Sam opened one of the pizza boxes. It was empty except for a few uneaten pizza crusts. Sam pinched the bread to see how fresh it was. It was still slightly dough-y. Someone had been here very recently.

Sam looked down the length of the mobile home. From

where he was standing, he could see the long, dark hallway, but he couldn't make anything out. The moonlight wasn't strong enough to cast any kind of glow down the corridor. If anything, it made the shadows even darker.

Suddenly, Sam heard a noise. It was faint. Just a single small creak. The unmistakable sound of a step on an old floor. He pointed his gun down the hallway.

"Who's there?" he shouted. "Norm, is that you?"

Sam stared into the darkness, looking for any sign of life.

"I don't want to hurt you," Sam continued. "Your wife sent me."

He immediately wondered if that was the best association he should have made, given the fact that Norm was hiding from his wife.

"I'm here to help you," Sam said as he took a step forward.

He thought he noticed some movement, but before he could even react, a blast from a rifle shattered the darkness.

37

THE SLIGHTLY MUFFLED SOUNDS OF LIVE MUSIC COULD BE HEARD from a block away, which is where Carla had to park her car. It was a classic Bob Seger song and, under normal circumstances, Carla would sing along. But tonight she barely even noticed it.

She walked through the doors of The Dive In, and the music immediately came to life. The bar was jammed with people and the band was rocking. Carla pushed her way through the crowd, not even sure what — or who — she was looking for. When she had texted back to the cryptic message she had received earlier, the only response she received simply said:

DON'T TELL ANYONE. ASK FOR CICI.

Carla finally maneuvered her way to the server station where a tall brunette in a Lemonheads tee-shirt was collecting drinks from the bartender.

"Excuse me," Carla yelled over the music. "Do you know where I can find Cici?"

The waitress smirked and looked at the bartender. Carla turned to see the bleached blonde woman looking at her.

"You must be Carla," Cici yelled, extending her hand. "I'm Cici."

She walked around the end of the bar so she was next to Carla.

"Thanks for coming," she said loudly. "We can talk in the back."

She motioned at a set of double swinging doors behind her that appeared to lead to a kitchen.

Carla nodded and Cici waved her hand to get the attention of a rough-looking guy bussing tables.

"Cover for me," she yelled to the guy as she motioned for Carla to follow her.

They walked through the small kitchen to a smaller room. Inside, a young woman, probably in her mid-20s, seemed to be waiting for them. She was sitting on a bar stool next to a desk that was pushed up against the wall. The stool and desk were the only two pieces of furniture in the room.

"Hey, Roxy," Cici said. "This is her."

Roxy introduced herself as one of the dayshift bartenders at the tavern.

Cici sat on the edge of the desk and Roxy offered Carla the stool.

"I'll stand. Thank you," Carla said, unsure what was going on.

Roxy shrugged and sat back down.

"Did you send me the text?" Carla asked.

"I did," Cici said. "Sorry about the cloak and dagger shit. And sorry for being all stalk-y. It's just that, Sam had mentioned you and I did a little digging and found your number. I didn't know how else to reach you without your sister knowing."

"Why can't my sister know?" Carla asked.

"Roxy here confided in me something she had heard. Something that may or may not come to light. About your sister," Cici explained. "I wasn't sure whether to tell Sam, and I sure as hell wasn't going to tell Detective Turner. But I figured I could share it with you and you could decide what to do."

Carla nodded, wondering what could be so bad that she was wondering whether or not to keep it a secret.

"Tell her what you told me," Cici said to Roxy.

"I'll just come out with it," Roxy said. "Your sister had an affair with John Rowe about a year ago. That's Jane's boyfriend."

"Yes, I know who he is," Carla said, still processing what the young bartender had just told her.

"It didn't last long," Roxy said. "It was during one of their 'separations.' And when Norm came back, the affair ended."

Carla was in shock. Vanessa had an affair? Carla had to force herself to stay engaged in the conversation.

"She just called it quits when Norm returned?" she asked.

"Well, kind of. They actually got caught. By Jane," Roxy answered. "Jane and John were already dating, so he was cheating, too."

"Holy shit," Carla said as she leaned back against the wall.

Roxy stood and once again offered Carla the bar stool. This time she took it.

"What made it worse was that Jane and Vanessa had been pretty good friends up to that point," Cici interjected.

Vanessa never told me she and Jane had been friends, thought Carla.

"I guess Jane eventually forgave John, since they were an item again. But she felt really betrayed by Vanessa," Roxy said.

"Did Norm know?" Carla asked.

"He must have found out," Roxy answered. "But he took Vanessa back anyway. And then somehow Jane and Norm became friends through the whole thing.

"I'm guessing Sam already filled you in on my theories about that," Cici said.

Carla nodded as she tried to catch up with all the information that had just been dumped on her.

"Anyway, they managed to keep the whole thing relatively quiet, so there was no big scandal," Roxy said. "But Jane and Vanessa never got along again."

Carla shook her head.

"Wait. How do you know all of this?" she asked, her voice angrier than she meant for it to be. "It sounds like small town gossip to me."

Roxy looked at Cici.

"I'm sure it does," Cici said. "But Roxy got it straight from the horses' mouths."

"I heard it from John," Roxy explained. "I can't imagine it's the kind of gossip he'd want to start."

"Why did he tell you?"

Roxy shrugged. "Bartender's curse."

"And why are you telling me this now?" Carla asked. "Are you saying my sister killed Jane because they were mad at each other?"

Cici shook her head.

"God, no," she said. "It's just that...I don't know your sister that well, but I know she's your sister. I have a sister, too. And if you're anything like me, we can get pretty protective."

"I don't understand," Carla said.

"This is the kind of shit some ambitious lawyer would throw out in court. Or leak to the press," Cici said. "And I guarantee you John would absolutely throw your sister under the bus if it would help keep him out of jail. I just didn't want you to be blind-sided by it. I figured if you knew, you could plan for it."

Carla felt the heat on her face and she took deep breaths to calm herself.

"I hope I wasn't out of line," Cici said.

"No," Carla said, shaking her head. "I'm just in shock. But I appreciate it."

Carla stood and let out a heavy sigh.

"You okay?" Roxy asked. "You don't look so hot."

Carla shook her head.

"I'm just realizing how little I know about my sister."

38

SAM LEAPT INTO THE KITCHEN, OUT OF SIGHT FROM THE HALLWAY. Pumped with adrenaline, he felt around for a wound and was relieved that he didn't seem to be bleeding.

"I'm sorry!" the man yelled from the shadows.

Sam could hear what sounded like a rifle being dropped to the floor. He leaned forward, toppling the table on its side and using it for cover.

"I didn't mean to do that," the man yelled.

Sam lifted up from behind the table, his gun pointing into the darkness.

"Come out where I can see you with your hands up," Sam yelled.

"Don't shoot me," the man pleaded. "I put the gun down."

Sam's ears were ringing from the rifle blast, but he could still hear the man walking slowly toward him.

"Where's the fucking lights?" Sam yelled.

"Right behind you on the wall," the man said.

Sam stood slowly, his pistol aimed at the darkness as he fumbled for the light switch. When he flipped it, both men flinched at the brightness. He looked at the man standing in front of him with his hands over his head.

It was Norm Mayhew.

Wearing a dirty T-shirt and cargo shorts, the barrel-chested man looked like he just stepped off a fishing boat. His short, light brown hair desperately needed a comb and he looked like he hadn't shaved in several days. Or slept, for that matter.

"Please don't shoot," Norm said.

"What the hell, Norm?" Sam yelled, double-checking to make sure he wasn't shot.

"How do you know my name?" Norm asked.

Sam let out a groan and walked toward Norm slowly, never dropping his pistol.

Where was Jude? He wondered. *Surely he heard the rifle blast.*

Sam turned Norm around and frisked him.

"Please don't kill me," Norm said.

"I'm not gonna hurt you," Sam said. "I'm here to help."

"Who are you?" Norm said as Sam spun him around so they faced each other.

Sam explained who he was, how he knew Vanessa and why he was there. He decided not to tell Norm that his father was with him. He had remembered what Jude had told him about Norm probably not reacting well to his presence.

"Is Nessie okay?" Norm asked.

"She's a little pissed off at you," Sam said sarcastically. "First the two of you have a lover's quarrel that sends you running, then you don't come back, and then you go and kill someone. What do you think?"

"I didn't kill anybody," he mumbled.

"Well, you're not acting very innocent," Sam said. "Innocent people don't hide out in dark trailer homes."

"I swear I didn't do it," Norm said.

Sam wasn't convinced. Almost every guilty person he'd ever

met had claimed they were innocent, sometimes even when they were caught red-handed.

"I hadn't even talked to Jane in over a week, much less seen her," Norm said.

Sam told him he knew about the texts Norm sent on the night she was murdered.

"Yeah, but she never answered," Norm said. "She hadn't answered for weeks."

"So you decided to confront her in person," Sam said. "And things got out of hand."

Norm shook his head.

"No. I'd been drinking and wasn't thinking straight," Norm said. "Jane used to be able to talk me down. She was a good friend. Gave me advice about how to deal with Vanessa."

"If she was such a good friend, then why was she ignoring your calls?" Sam said. "And don't try my patience. I'm still pretty pissed you shot at me."

"I told you I was sorry," Norm said. "And I don't know why she started ignoring me. Maybe John found out we were talking and got pissed. I don't know. And, yeah. I did go to her house that night. I'd been drinking and was in a dark place. I needed to talk."

"Well, you had a wife about a mile away," Sam replied. "You ever think of talking to her?"

"Not while I was drinking," Norm said.

"So, instead you go to the house of a woman you'd had an affair with," Sam said.

Norm shook his head.

"No. It's more complicated than that," Norm said.

"You can see why I'm having trouble believing you," Sam said.

"But it's the truth," Norm said. "I went to her house. It was about 1:00 in the morning. The door was open, so I knew something was wrong. Then I saw her lying there. And then all the blood."

Norm clenched his eyes shut, trying to push away the memory.

"Did you see who did it?" Sam said.

Norm looked at Sam in fear, shaking his head nervously.

"No. I didn't see anyone."

Sam could tell he was lying.

"I don't believe you, Norman," Sam said.

"I swear," Norm insisted. "You have to believe me."

"Why didn't you call 9-1-1?" Sam asked, shifting gears.

"I couldn't," Norm said. "I know how it sounds, but I was drunk and in shock and I just...ran."

Sam studied Norm's face. He wasn't sure whether he was a really good liar or just a pathetic weasel. He also didn't look like someone capable of committing such a violent act. Still, something about his story just wasn't sitting right.

"I need you to come back with me," Sam said.

Norm shook his head vehemently. "No," he said. "I can't."

"Look, I got here first but your buddy Paul Turner is probably going to figure out you're here soon enough," Sam said. "It'll look much better if you come in on your own."

"I can't," Norm said. "You don't understand."

"Then just tell me," Sam said. "Who did you see there?"

Norm shook his head.

"I can't."

"Did they threaten you?" Sam asked. "I can protect you. But I can't do anything if you don't help me out here."

Norm sighed, realizing he didn't really have a choice. He nodded and was about to tell Sam, but a look of fear suddenly swept over his face. Before Sam could turn to see what had caused the reaction, he felt a sharp pain crack through his skull.

And then everything went black.

39

CARLA'S STOMACH WAS IN KNOTS AS SHE WALKED BACK INTO THE house. It was dark, except for a warm golden glow from a light that hung over the kitchen table. Carla went into the kitchen and mindlessly poured herself a glass of water. She was still trying to come to terms with what she had just learned.

As flighty and free-spirited as her sister could be, Carla had never seen her as a person who would sneak around—for any reason. Granted, it had happened when she and Norm were having one of their "sabbaticals." Not that she was excusing it, but she understood how it could happen.

But this wasn't about the affair. Carla was upset that her sister hadn't told her about her friendship with Jane, and the animosity that had developed between the two. There was so much that Vanessa hadn't told her. What else was she hiding?

Knowing that it would eat at her all night, and knowing that Sam and Jude were off looking for Norm, Carla decided that she couldn't wait until the morning to confront Vanessa.

She walked down the hall and knocked gently on Vanessa's door.

"Vanessa? Sorry to wake you," Carla said just loud enough to wake her sister without startling her. "Can I come in?"

She waited for her sister to respond, and when she didn't, she knocked a second time, but this time a little louder.

"Nessie?" she said loudly. "You up?"

She turned the door handle and cracked the door slightly.

"Hey, sorry to wake you," she said as she walked in the room.

But she froze in shock when she saw that Vanessa's bed was empty.

"Nessie?" Carla called out.

She flipped on the light just to be sure, but Vanessa was definitely not in the room. Carla rushed down the hall, hoping her sister had just gone to the bathroom. But the bathroom door was open, and the room was empty.

"Vanessa?" Carla yelled out, her heart pumping.

Where had her sister gone?

She ran outside to the garage that was set away from the house. Vanessa's car was gone.

Carla ran back to the house, pulling out her phone and calling Vanessa. She listened to it ring until finally going to voicemail. She left a quick message asking her sister to call her and then, as soon as she hung up, she noticed the note on the kitchen counter for the first time. Without even reading it, Carla felt a wave of relief wash over her. If there was a note, then at least her sister had left on her own.

She turned on the kitchen light and grabbed the piece of paper, instantly recognizing Vanessa's handwriting.

WHERE ARE YOU?

I COULDN'T SLEEP SO I WENT TO THE BEACH. BE BACK LATER. DON'T WAIT UP!

Relieved and feeling slightly silly for her paranoia, Carla put down the note. Still, why hadn't her sister tried to call her? And why didn't she answer her phone now?

Carla realized she was suspicious of her sister.

Realizing she had the house to herself, Carla decided to look around a bit. They had already torn the house apart looking for clues regarding Norm's whereabouts, but were there things that Vanessa had been hiding from Carla? She replayed their searches over in her mind and remembered that Vanessa had done most of the looking in her bedroom.

Carla snooped around in her sister's bedroom. She rifled through the drawers of the dresser, then checked the shelves in the closet, feeling guilty the entire time. It reminded her of her childhood, when she would check her sister's room for missing clothes that Vanessa had "borrowed."

Prompted by the nostalgia, Carla recalled her sister's favorite hiding place: between the mattress and box spring of her bed. Dropping to her knees, Carla slid her hands under the mattress and felt around. When her hands touched something metal, she froze.

Her heart pounded as she realized what she had found. Grabbing it by the handle, she slowly pulled it out.

A large chef's knife.

Her mind spun in a million directions, but she was yanked out of her shock by the approach of car lights in the driveway.

40

CARLA SHOVED THE KNIFE BACK UNDER THE MATTRESS AND RACED out of the bedroom, making it to the kitchen just as Vanessa opened the door. She looked startled to see her sister waiting for her.

"There you are," Carla stammered.

Carla couldn't help but notice that Vanessa seemed disoriented and more than a little disheveled. Vanessa seemed to notice the way her sister was looking at her and attempted to straighten her hair with her hand.

"I must look like a mess," she said. "The wind was really strong out on the beach."

"I was worried," Carla said.

"Didn't you see my note?" Vanessa asked.

"I called, but you didn't answer," Carla replied.

Vanessa smiled. "I left my phone in the car," she said. "By the time I realized, I didn't want to walk all the way back. I'm sorry. But you know you ran out on me first. Where were you?"

"Sam asked me to follow up on something for him," Carla lied. "You were already in bed. Asleep, I thought. I didn't want to bother you."

Vanessa smiled and nodded, but didn't respond otherwise. Carla couldn't decide if her sister seemed disoriented and preoccupied or if she was just reading too much into things. But there were too many unanswered questions for her to not say something.

"We need to talk," Carla said.

"Can it possibly wait until morning?" Vanessa asked. "It's late and I'm bushed."

Carla grabbed Vanessa's arm as she tried to walk past her.

"No," Carla said. "We need to talk now."

Sensing the urgency in Carla's tone, Vanessa nodded and motioned for them both to move to the couch.

"You're not being honest with me," Carla said as she sat down. "I know you're not."

At first, Vanessa looked at her sister like she had no idea what she was talking about. But, realizing Carla could see right through the facade, she let out a sigh and nodded, looking down to avoid eye contact.

"You're right," she said.

She sat in silence, partly to muster up courage to talk, but also hoping that Carla would say something first to start the conversation. But Carla wasn't saying a word. She wanted to hear her sister's confession without any assistance.

"I lied to you," Vanessa finally said. "And Sam."

Carla nodded, expecting her sister to admit to the affair and the animosity between Jane and herself. She was caught off guard when Vanessa finally spoke.

"I knew about the mobile home," she said. "I mean, I had forgotten about it. But when Sam showed me the lease, it all came back."

It took a second for Carla to bring herself around to Vanessa's confession.

"That's your lie?" she asked. "Why would you lie about that?"

Vanessa shrugged. "I honestly don't know," she said. "Partly out of embarrassment, partly out of feeling protective over Norm."

She explained that, as soon as she saw the lease, she knew Norm was probably hiding there. She had hoped if she downplayed it, Sam would just drop it.

"But then I realized Sam was too good a cop for that," she said. "He wasn't going to just let it go. And then I thought, maybe he was Norm's best bet. If Detective Turner knew about the mobile home, he'd probably go in guns blazing. And, at that point, I figured it didn't matter if I knew about it."

"You didn't just lie about it," Carla said. "You put on a whole show. I sat here with you as you pretended to be angry at Norm for having this double life. You lied to me over. And over. And over."

Vanessa nodded. "I'm really sorry, Carla. I don't know what to say."

Carla grabbed her sister's hands and looked her dead in the eyes.

"Is there anything else you need to tell me?" she asked.

Vanessa pulled her hands free and took a deep breath before she spoke.

41

SAM WOKE UP, LYING ON THE FLOOR OF THE MOBILE HOME, A burning pain shooting through his skull from the back of his head. A deafening ring filled his ears and everything was dark and blurry.

"Hello?" he called out, trying to remember where he was.

There was no answer.

He touched the back of his head. Luckily, there was no blood. Still, there was a massive goose egg where someone must have hit him.

He grimaced in pain as he tried to put the pieces together of what had happened. Where was he? Who had hit him?

Using the toppled folding table as leverage, he tried to pull himself up but fell back on his hands and knees. He needed a second to pull himself together. He waited for the room to spin more slowly and the ringing in his ears to fade. He began to notice the familiar muffled sounds of a wind chime.

He looked around the dark room, squinting to bring anything into focus.

There was something on the other side of the room.

He squinted harder. There was definitely something there. Or was it someone?

His memories started to come back. He had been talking to someone. But he couldn't remember who.

He looked back at the object on the other side of the room. It was definitely a person.

"Hey," he said. "You okay?"

The words pierced through his head and echoed. His mind began to slowly focus and things started to come back to him. He remembered he had been talking to Norm. He had found Norm at a mobile home and they had been talking when someone hit him over the head.

The memory of the attack caused a sharp pain to crash through his head.

"Norm?" he asked. "Is that you?"

Remembering he had a cell phone, Sam pulled it from the back pocket of his jeans and tapped the screen, sending a faint blue glow over the room.

Sam turned the screen toward the person lying across from him. From his angle, he couldn't make out the face.

All he could see was blood.

"Norm? You okay?"

He started to crawl toward the body but, just before he could get there, the door to the mobile home burst open. Sam looked up and tried to focus on the intruder. The man leaned down to check on Sam. It was Jude.

"What happened?" Jude asked.

He was out of breath and Sam thought he saw a trickle of blood on Jude's forehead.

"Where were you?" Sam asked.

"Someone clocked me from behind," Jude muttered, clearly embarrassed.

"Yeah, same here," Sam said. "Did you get a look at him?"

"I heard a shot," Jude interrupted.

But before Sam could answer, Jude's attention had already shifted to the other body in the room.

"Jude," Sam said, trying to stop him.

It was too late.

Jude stepped slowly toward the body, then fell to his knees, crying out in despair.

42

SAM BRUSHED OFF THE PARAMEDIC TENDING TO HIS HEAD WOUND and went back inside the mobile home, which was swarming with police. Less than five minutes after Sam called 911, patrol cars from Dennis, along with the Massachusetts State Police, had arrived. Sam looked around for the detective he had spoken to earlier to see what they had found, but before he could utter a word, Turner stormed into the mobile home.

"Damnit, Sam," he yelled. "What the hell did you do?"

Sam winced at the loud voice. His head was still throbbing. He held up his hand to motion for Turner to keep it down.

Turner walked past Sam to look at Norm's bloodied body lying on the floor. Sam walked up next to him. Turner spun around to face Sam.

"I should arrest you right now," he yelled. "What the hell were you thinking?"

"What are you doing here?" Sam asked.

"Local cops called me after talking to you," Turner answered. "I know you think we don't know what we're doing, but we've been looking for Norm for over a week."

Sam nodded. It made perfect sense they would call Turner.

Now Sam just had to make sure that he didn't fan the flames and make things worse.

"I just wanted to check first..." he started to explain.

"You just wanted to check if Norm was here?" Turner interrupted. "So you and his dad could help him escape?"

"I was just following up on a theory," Sam snapped back. "I didn't think he'd really be here."

Turner ignored him, asking for someone to fill him in. A forensics technician who was kneeling near Norm's body spoke up.

"The victim was shot three times at point blank range," he said in a monotone voice, like he was giving a book report. "From the blood splatters, it looks like the first bullet hit him dead between the eyes while he was standing. The other two shots were fired into his chest after he was on the ground. Probably just to make sure he was dead."

"When I was attacked, he was sitting across from me over there. In that chair," Sam said, pointing to a kitchen chair that was lying on its side next to the table.

"What about a weapon?" Turner asked the technician, still ignoring Sam.

Sam winced in advance of what was coming.

"Can't find the weapon," the technician said, glancing at Sam. "But we did find some 40 S&W cartridges."

"That's police standard," Turner said to himself.

"Probably my gun," Sam interrupted.

Turner spun around to Sam.

"What?" he asked.

"My gun's missing," Sam continued, somewhat sheepishly. "I'm guessing our killer knocked me out and then took my gun."

"You've got to be shitting me," Turner said.

Sam shook his head. "I wish I was."

Turner let out a groan and paced around in circles.

"You realize what this looks like," Turner said.

"Oh, please," Sam said. "You think I clocked Jude then shot Norm then hid a gun that's easily traceable to me and then knocked myself out?"

"How does anyone know you were unconscious?" Turner retorted. "There're no witnesses to that. That's just your story. For all I know, you shot Norm in a fit of anger, then staged the whole assault to cover it up."

"That's a bullshit theory and you know it," Sam said. "And what about Jude? Whoever did this got to him, too."

Turner looked out the open trailer door and saw Jude sitting on a lawn chair, his head in his hands.

"That poor man had to see his dead son like this, because of you," Turner said.

"He insisted on coming," Sam said. "In fact, he talked me into coming here without calling you. My vote was to call you. For the record."

"No man should see their son that way," Turner said.

The local detective, an overweight man in his fifties wearing a golf shirt and khakis, trudged over. He was breathing heavy through his nose and Sam worried he would fall over from a heart attack on the spot. The man shook Turner's hand, and the two walked away from Sam to trade notes. Sam looked out at Jude. He felt he should go say something to comfort the poor guy, but what could he possibly say? Instead, Sam redirected his attention to the investigation and tried to eavesdrop on the conversation between the two detectives.

"The fact that the perp left Mr. Lawson and Mr. Mayhew alive would indicate that the victim here was the sole target," the overweight detective said. "Plus, if the weapon was his stolen sidearm as he claims, the perp didn't arrive with a weapon."

"Who shows up to kill someone without a weapon?" Sam asks loudly.

"Someone who wasn't planning on killing anyone," Turner snapped back before pulling the local detective further away from Sam.

Sam knew that, of course. But he never met a wise crack he couldn't pass up. In truth, he was actually relieved to know that he wasn't really a suspect. He knew if he were investigating this case, he would consider himself a person of interest.

Turner walked back over.

"Two murders in two days and, somehow, you were there alone with both bodies before the cops arrived," Turner said.

"Come on, Paul," Sam said, growing impatient with the harassment. "You know I didn't do it."

"I know that you probably led the killer right to Norm. Hell, you even gave him the murder weapon," Turner said.

"What's your point?" Sam asked.

"Norm was clearly hiding from someone," Turner said

"He was hiding from you," Sam snapped back, getting in Turner's face.

The local detective inserted himself between Sam and Turner.

"If you two fellas are going to argue, at least take it outside," he said. "This is a crime scene."

Sam nodded. "I should probably get him back," he said, motioning toward Jude.

Wanting to help the grieving father was something the two men had in common, and their feud immediately faded.

"Ferrys aren't running this late," Turner said. "I can take you both back on the Coast Guard vessel."

Sam nodded. Then sank into himself with a second realization.

"Shit," he said.

"What now?" Turner asked.

"One of us needs to tell Vanessa her husband's been murdered."

43

As the Coast Guard boat cut across Vineyard Sound, Turner, Sam and Jude travelled in silence. The sun was beginning to rise and a brilliant band of yellow cut across the ocean's horizon, fading into blue then purple. Under any other circumstances it would have been breathtaking, but the three men barely noticed. And certainly didn't care.

Even as Turner drove Jude and Sam to Vanessa's house, no one spoke a word. At first, it was out of respect for Jude's grief. Then, as time passed, and no one knew what to say, they had all fallen into the safety of quietude. For Jude and Turner, silence was easy. Sam was having a tougher time with it. There had been many times that he had wanted to crack a joke or make some sort of sarcastic comment to ease the awkwardness. But every time, he had looked at Jude's forlorn face and thought better of it.

However, as the tires crunched over Vanessa's driveway, he needed to speak up out of necessity.

"So who's going to tell her?" he asked.

"I am," Jude said, his voice cracking as he spoke.

Turner knocked on the door loudly. When there was no answer, he started to knock a second time, but Jude grabbed his hand to stop him. He stepped between the two men and reached up over the doorsill, pulling down a key and unlocking the door.

The three men entered just as Carla and Vanessa were approaching the door. From their matted hair and puffy eyes, they had clearly both been asleep but now shared the same concerned look.

"Was he there?" Vanessa asked.

She stopped when she realized the somber expressions on all three men's faces. Jude took a step forward.

"Nessie," he said, his voice not much louder than a whisper.

Vanessa put her hand on the couch to steady herself. Carla stepped closer to support her.

"I'm so sorry," Jude continued.

Vanessa immediately crumbled, and Carla grabbed her to keep her from falling to the ground. Sam and Turner both ran over to help and the three of them led her to the couch and helped her sit down.

Jude walked over and sat on the coffee table directly across from Vanessa. He took her hands in his and a lone tear ran down his cheek. He attempted to speak, but couldn't find the words. He didn't have to. Vanessa leaned forward and put her arms around her father-in-law, sobbing into his shoulder. That was all it took to melt the stoic facade Jude had forced on himself. He leaned forward, holding Vanessa tight as they cried into each other's arms.

Feeling he was spying on an intimate moment, Sam looked over at Carla. She was looking at her sister, but not with a look of compassion as he would expect. She looked concerned.

44

"THERE'S NO WAY MY SISTER COULD DO ANYTHING LIKE THAT," Carla whispered loudly.

She and Sam were walking in the sand of Lucy Vincent Beach on a cool, cloudy morning. It had been a couple of hours since the men had returned with the bad news about Norm. Turner had driven Jude home and Vanessa, after taking a sedative, finally fell asleep.

But Sam was too wound up to go to sleep and Carla suggested they get out of the house to talk through everything that happened. Sam went into more detail about Norm's death than had been told in front of Vanessa, and Carla told Sam about her discovery of Vanessa's affair with John, her bad relationship with Jane and, more importantly, the discovery of the knife.

"She doesn't strike me as the stabby kind," Sam agreed. "Still..."

"Still what?" Carla asked.

"Maybe she has a violent temper you don't know about," Sam suggested. "Maybe she snuck over to Jane's while you were asleep, thinking she'd find Norm there. Instead, she and Jane got into an argument and things got out of hand."

Carla shook her head. "I can't even picture it."

"Maybe Norm caught her in the act," he continued. "Or he walked in while Vanessa was still standing over the body. Maybe Vanessa threatened him. Either way, he panicked and ran. Worked out good for Vanessa. Until we started closing in on him. Then she had to silence him."

"Do you really think she could stab someone fifteen times? Do you think she would kill her husband like that?" Carla argued. "That's the work of a cold-blooded killer."

"But, other than you and Jude, she's the only one who knew where I was," Sam said. "And she did seem to have conveniently disappeared during the time of the attack."

"I checked the ferry schedule," Carla said. "There's no way she could have got over there and back in the time she was gone."

Sam shrugged. "Maybe she didn't take the ferry."

"Well, there would be boat records or video footage from the harbors, right?" Carla asked. "Like there was with Norm?"

"Maybe," Sam said. "I'll see what I can find. But that detective has got me on a short leash. I'm probably gonna have to go through him."

Carla nodded, and the two stopped to watch as large waves crashed into a large cluster of boulders on the shore.

"It is beautiful," Carla said.

"It's freezing," Sam said with a shiver. "Beaches are supposed to be warm. I should be in a bathing suit, not a jacket."

Carla smiled.

"It'll warm up in a month," she said.

"I still wouldn't get in that water," Sam said. "You put your foot in it? You'll get frostbite."

"But it's gorgeous," Carla said.

"I'll be just fine looking at a postcard then," Sam teased. "While I'm sitting on my warm beach."

Carla laughed, but the smile quickly faded as her mind drifted back to more pressing matters.

"What do you think about the knife?" Carla asked.

"There was no blood on it?" Sam asked.

"No," Carla said. "But even the coldest killer is going to wash a knife off before they hide it."

"There could be some trace DNA still on it," Sam asked. "We need to get it. But to be admissible, we need to be careful how we retrieve it."

"Meaning?" Carla asked.

"Meaning you can 'accidentally' find it as you're making your sister's bed and bring it into the station," he answered. "If I am anywhere near it, Turner is gonna smell a rat and a DA could argue it was an illegal search."

They walked in silence for a bit. The pink morning clouds had faded into a light blue and birds began to sing and chirp. Under any other circumstance, it would have been a beautiful morning.

"I feel like my sister's hiding something," Carla said. "But I don't believe she's capable of murder."

"We can't forget about one other thing," Sam said.

"Oh God," Carla said. "What else?"

"The only four people that knew about the trip to the mobile home were you, me, Vanessa...and Jude."

Carla looked at Sam to see if he was inferring what she thought he was.

"He said he heard the rifle blast but got knocked out when he fell," Sam said. "Then showed up after everything had happened."

"That's Norm's father," Carla argued.

Sam shrugged again.

"I've seen family members do some pretty cold-blooded things," Sam said. "We have to explore every possibility."

"You don't really think Jude did it, do you?" Carla asked.

"*Every* possibility," Sam repeated.

As they walked back to the house, they mapped out a list of suspects and the pros and cons of each. They decided they'd both try to get a few hours of sleep and then dig deeper on a few things.

"We never got that mattress," Sam suddenly remembered.

"We can flip a coin for the couch," Carla said.

Sam was about to suggest they share the couch when he was interrupted by the ringing of his phone. He looked at the Caller ID and his face immediately fell.

45

"Hey, Chief," he said into the phone. "You're up awfully early."

"What the hell are you doing?" Chief Bannon yelled into the phone. "Why the hell am I getting calls from the Chilmark Police Department at four in the morning?"

Sam's stomach dropped. Bannon was the Quinton Police Chief and very open about his disdain for Sam. In fact, the only reason he let Sam take the days off on such short notice was because he'd rather be short-handed than have to look at Sam's face. And now he was probably calling because Turner complained about him. Rather than jump straight on the defensive, Sam did what he always did. Play dumb.

"Chilmark PD? From here on Martha's Vineyard?" Sam asked, trying to sound shocked. "Why would they be calling you?"

"Cut the bullshit, Lawson," Bannon snapped. "You know better than to interfere with local investigations."

"Interfere?" Sam asked, abandoning the dumb ploy immediately. "I've been helping them. Look, it's this one detective. He has it out for me and..."

"Did you or did you not conceal the whereabouts of a wanted fugitive from them?" Bannon interrupted.

"I just wanted to be sure he was there first," Sam said.

"Did you or did you not let someone steal your police-issued firearm?" Bannon continued. "A weapon you should not have had on you while on vacation."

"I didn't *let* them," Sam argued.

"Did or did not your direct, unwanted involvement in this case contribute to the death of the fugitive?" Bannon asked.

Sam felt his blood beginning to boil. His anger wasn't directed at Bannon. He was always an asshole. Sam was pissed at Turner for tattling on him like a whiny schoolkid.

"I also got a concerned call from Bobby Lyons yesterday," Bannon said.

Sam let out a groan. Bobby was the dispatcher he had asked to do the background check on John Rowe.

"Apparently you requested a criminal check on a local resident?" Bannon asked.

"I had reason to believe he was involved with this murder," Sam argued back.

"You are not on duty," Bannon said. "Again, your help is not welcome by the local authorities. I don't need the Chilmark Chief of Police calling me at 4 in the morning to demand I get control of one of my men—who is supposedly on vacation."

So it wasn't Turner, Sam thought. Still, he must've complained to his chief, and that's who ratted him out. He was still responsible.

"I told them they have my full support and I would not stand in the way if they want to arrest you for hindering their investigation," Bannon said. "In fact, I encouraged it."

"Thanks, boss," Sam sneered back. "Glad to see you have my back."

"I'll have your badge if you interfere again, you understand?"

Bannon hung up before Sam could argue back, which was probably best. Anything else Sam said would have probably got him suspended on the spot.

He put down the phone and looked at Carla.

"I'm guessing you heard all of that," he said.

She nodded.

"Maybe we should just let Detective Turner do his job," she said. "I don't want you to get in any more trouble over this."

"If Turner wanted to arrest me, he already would have," Sam said. "And if Bannon suspends me, I'll..."

He stopped to think about what his reaction would be. He was getting tired of Bannon always breathing down his neck. But Sam had a similar problem with his last chief. In fact, he'd always fought with his superiors. Clearly, he had a problem with authority.

"If he wants to suspend me, I'll quit."

46

JUDE PULLED UP TO THE POLICE STATION JUST AS TURNER WAS walking out the door. It was late afternoon, and the detective had spent the bulk of the day at the murder scene in Dennis.

"Paul, can I have a minute?" Jude said as he stepped out of his truck.

Turner hadn't even noticed Jude until he spoke. It had been a long day, and all he wanted to do was go home and get some sleep, but he couldn't exactly just walk away from the father of a murder victim.

"It won't take long," Jude said. "Please."

It was a nice day and Turner didn't want to go back in the police station. There was too much that could keep him there. He pointed to a bench in the park next to the station and the two men walked in silence toward it.

Turner could tell Jude hadn't slept either. But he was also clearly overcome with grief. His eyes were bloodshot, but also empty. He seemed pale and even weak—two words no one would ever use to describe Jude Mayhew.

The men sat down. Turner knew it was best to wait until Jude was ready to talk.

"You've got a boy, right?" Jude finally said, looking at the ground in front of him.

Turner nodded. "Yes, sir," he said. "Just turned five."

Jude forced a weak smile.

"That's a good age. A fun age," he said. "Savor every minute of it."

Turner shifted uncomfortably on the bench. He felt sorry for this grieving father, but was really too tired to listen to him wax philosophically about appreciating your child. Besides, Turner had already been thinking about his own son all day.

"You know the first thing that hits you when family dies?" Jude asked. "All the things you regret not saying to them. Or doing with them."

Turner nodded. He knew Jude wasn't looking for a response. He just needed someone to talk to.

"I was hard on Norm," Jude said. "But he needed it. I had to be his rudder, even when it bordered on cruel. That's what a father has to do."

He stooped down on one knee and picked up a small rock, twirling it between his fingers.

"What I regret is that I never told him how proud I was of him," he continued. "And despite everything, I really was."

His voice trailed off as he tried to push down his emotions.

"Regrets are like ghosts," he said. "They'll haunt you forever and there's nothing you can do about it."

He turned to face Turner for the first time.

"I don't want you to have regrets," he said.

Turner was confused. He wasn't sure where the conversation was going.

"I don't either," Turner said. "I try to be a good dad."

Jude shook his head.

"Not just about your son," he said. "Regrets about anything. About this investigation."

Turner let out a sigh. He saw where this was going. Lawson must have sent him.

"Look, I need you to know that I'm doing everything I can to find your son's killer," he said. "And Jane Caplan's killer. I'm just asking you to be patient."

"Sam Lawson is a good man," Jude said. "And you could use his help."

"That man is sabotaging everything," Turner said. "He should have told me about the mobile home. Frankly, Jude, you should have told me."

Jude nodded.

"I suppose," he said. "But Sam was pretty sure it was a dead end."

"Guess he's not such a great detective after all," Turner snapped. "And regardless, that's not his decision to make. I can forgive you. Norm's your son and you were acting out of emotion. But Sam's a cop. He should know better. And now your son is dead because of him."

He saw the way Jude winced at the statement, and he immediately regretted his choice of words.

"I should have been there," Jude muttered. "If I wouldn't have tripped..."

Jude's voice trailed off as he buried his feelings deep.

"You can't blame yourself," Turner said with a gentler tone. "That was all Sam's doing. He should have called me."

"What would have been different if you had gone?" Jude said. "You'd have been the one hit over the head. That's all."

"I wouldn't have let anyone sneak up on me," Turner said.

Jude stared at the rock he was playing with, as if he was searching for the next thing to say.

"I know you and Norm had your differences. And you're entitled to your opinion of him," Jude said. "Norm was a son-of-a-bitch and a thorn in your side. But, you've got blinders on, son. And Sam could see that."

"Wait. So this is my fault?" Turner asked.

Jude clenched his jaw.

"Stop looking for someone to blame, and start looking for who did this," he snapped.

Turner took a second to collect himself before speaking.

"I'm a good cop, Mr. Mayhew," he said. "My team are good men. We are doing more than you are even aware of, and we're doing it by the book so that it stands up in court. But I can't be a policeman for this town and a babysitter of some bored cowboy."

"You're only one man," Jude countered quietly. "And you've never conducted a murder investigation. You could use the help and you've got an experienced cop offering to do just that."

Jude stood up and turned, looking down at Turner.

"If my son is a murderer, then so be it. But if he is innocent and you let him take the fall because of your pride, a lot of people are going to have a lot of regrets. You understand what I'm saying?"

Turner jumped up. "Are you threatening me?"

As soon as he spoke, he could see that Jude's eyes were filled with grief, not malice.

"I'm just saying I don't want you to look back on this case and regret you didn't do everything in your power to find the truth."

47

CARLA FOLLOWED VANESSA INTO THE TOWN OF OAK BLUFFS, trailing as far behind as she could without losing sight of her sister. She had been surprised that Vanessa had wanted to go out at all. Since Jude had identified the body the night before, she was spared that sadistic ritual. And even though Norm's body was going to have to stay in Woods Hole pending a complete autopsy, there were still funeral arrangements she needed to make. Carla had offered to go with her and was surprised when Vanessa refused her help. It was enough to make Carla suspicious enough to follow her.

Sam had gone with Jude back to the mainland to answer more questions. Luckily, he had left Norm's work truck at Vanessa's.

When Vanessa pulled into the parking lot of Welch's Funeral Home, Carla pulled over into a hardware store parking lot. She prayed Vanessa wouldn't see her. Not only would she not appreciate being followed, but seeing her recently dead husband's truck in her rear-view mirror could possibly trigger a heart attack.

Carla waited patiently, grateful that the dead fish smell

seemed to have mostly aired out of the truck's cab. Still, she was relieved when Vanessa emerged from the funeral home so she could start driving and run some fresh air through the open windows. She followed Vanessa through town until she arrived at a car repair shop. Carla parked at the end of the street, hidden from view by a thick rhododendron hedge. While it hid the truck, it still offered her a decent view of the front of the shop.

She watched Vanessa park her car in front of the silver metal warehouse building, and her heart pounded when she saw a man emerge from the shop's office door. She immediately recognized his face from the criminal record she had read with Sam.

It was John Rowe.

Vanessa got out of her car and the two began talking. Vanessa was crying and John offered a consoling hug. They spoke some more and John reached up and wiped a tear from her face.

Carla's stomach turned. She felt dizzy. She tried to think of a million excuses that would give her sister the benefit of the doubt.

John nodded in agreement to something and the two hugged once more before Vanessa got back in her car and drove away. A stunned Carla started to follow and almost pulled out right in front of passing traffic. She hit the brakes hard and let the car pass. It was just enough time for Vanessa to disappear from sight.

Carla groaned in frustration and sat back to figure out her next move. Looking back at the garage, she saw another car pull into the parking lot. And she gasped when she recognized the woman who stepped out of it.

48

It was Gina. The nurse who had told Carla about Jane's pregnancy.

What a small world, thought Carla. *Then again, there probably aren't too many auto mechanics on the island. Plus, if Gina was Jane's best friend, she surely knew John.*

Gina was wearing her nurse scrubs and was all smiles as she almost skipped up to John, who was still standing in the parking lot. She said something to him and he nodded, grinning from ear to ear, watching as Gina walked past him and inside the office door. John looked around and then followed, flipping the OPEN sign over so it read CLOSED.

Carla could feel her curiosity getting the best of her. She quickly rationalized Gina's presence and even the fact that they went into his shop and locked the door. After all, they were both grieving over the loss of Jane. Although, from both of their smiles, neither seemed particularly grief-stricken. Before she even really thought about it, Carla found herself getting out of the truck to get a better look.

Luckily, there were no windows on the front of the shop, so Carla didn't have to worry about being seen as she walked up the road. Still, she walked lightly and weaved behind bushes and cars. Just to be safe. She quietly snuck around to the side of the shop in hopes of finding a window or an open door, and was relieved to see one about halfway down the building.

She crouched below the window and lifted her head slowly to look inside. The room was dimly lit, except for several shop lights over three cars in various states of disrepair. Carla craned her neck to see if she could see the office, but rows of auto parts and tools were blocking her view.

Then she heard a woman laughing and saw Gina walk out of the office towards one car. It was a red sports car similar to the Mustang Sam had back in Texas. Gina leaned on the trunk of the car and looked toward the office, motioning for John to join her.

John walked over and stood in front of her as the two talked and laughed. Then Gina put her hands around John's neck and pulled him toward her. He pressed against her as the two locked in a passionate kiss.

Carla's jaw hit the floor. These two were clearly more than friends, and they were clearly not grieving. She watched a second longer, just long enough to see Gina start kissing down John's chest until she dropped to her knees in front of him.

49

SAM WALKED OUT ON THE RESTAURANT'S SECOND FLOOR DECK, which looked out over Oak Bluffs Harbor. It was one of a string of restaurants along the harbor that Sam imagined was packed with people in the busy summer months. But right now, there were only a handful of people, including Carla, who was waiting at the bar. She had called him earlier and asked if he could return to the island as soon as possible. Sensing the urgency in her voice, he and Jude returned as quickly as they could and Jude had dropped Sam off.

He gave her a kiss and then motioned to the bartender to order a drink. Carla motioned for him to follow her to a table.

"What's going on that you couldn't tell me on the phone?" Sam asked.

Carla looked around to make sure no one was listening.

"I knew Jude or the police were going to be around you," Carla said. "I wanted to make sure this was just between you and me."

She then proceeded to tell Sam about what she had seen at John's Auto Shop. Sam took a second putting together all the pieces.

"Gina. That's the nurse that was Jane's best friend?" he asked.

Carla nodded.

"The one that told me about Jane's pregnancy," Carla said.

Talking excitedly but as quietly as possible, Carla told Sam her theory that John and Gina were having an affair. Maybe John was planning on breaking up with Jane. But then Jane got pregnant, which obviously complicated things. So John killed her to solve the problem.

"But then Norm walked in and caught him in the act," Sam said, picking up on the theory.

"That's why he was hiding," Carla said. "John was probably looking for him, and he finally caught up with him at the mobile home. He must have followed you."

The possibility that he had led a killer to Norm turned Sam's stomach, but it also strengthened his resolve to make sure the bastard didn't get away with it. He mulled the theory over in his head.

"What about your sister?" Sam asked. "You said she had disappeared."

"She went to the beach," Carla said.

"And the knife under her mattress? Here's a theory," Sam offered. "Your sister thought Norm and Jane were having an affair. She confronted Jane and things got out of hand. And in a fit of rage, she killed Jane. Unfortunately, Norm saw it. They were already having problems. He had abandoned her, so there was no love lost between them. She knew what she had to do to cover up her crime. But that was something she couldn't do on her own. She's not cold-blooded. So she hired John to do it."

Carla shook her head. "Why would she kill the man that she had just killed someone else over?"

Sam shrugged. "She panicked?" he asked. "People do some pretty messed up shit to cover up a crime of passion. Things they wouldn't normally do."

"Out of those two theories, which do you think is the most plausible?" Carla asked.

Sam thought about it.

"I don't know," he finally said. "But it doesn't really matter. Both roads lead to John Rowe."

He stood up.

"It's at least enough to bring to Turner," he said.

Sam could see Carla's surprise that he wanted to involve the detective.

"It's not like I'm going to make a citizen's arrest based on theory," he explained. "I've gotta go by the books at this point."

Carla also remembered the conversation Sam had with his boss.

"Sam, they've already complained about you once," she said. "If you involve yourself again, you're going to be putting your job at risk. Let me talk to Turner."

Sam grinned.

"And miss all the fun?" he teased. "Not on your life."

She started to protest, but Sam stopped her.

"I need to back off and let him take it from here," Sam said.

"And if he doesn't?" Carla asked.

Sam grinned.

"Then we fall to Plan B," he said, kissing Carla on the forehead. "But I've got to give Turner first shot at it."

"And I need to talk to my sister," Carla said.

50

VANESSA SAT ON THE COUCH, SIPPING HOT LAVENDER TEA FROM A mug. After her manic round of errands, she came home and realized she couldn't run from her reality any longer. Her world was different now. It was a hard adjustment to make. Vanessa had gotten used to feeling a sense of hope that he would return at any moment. That hope still lingered in her mind, and she had to keep reminding herself that hope was gone. Norm was never coming back.

Carla curled up next to her on the couch, sipping her own tea. She looked at her sister, wondering what thoughts were going through her head. She had always felt she knew her sister and now she felt like the woman sitting at the other end of the couch was a complete stranger.

"So what'd you do today?" Carla finally asked.

Vanessa was so deep in thought, it took a while for the words to pull her into reality.

"I had to go to the funeral home, pick up some supplies for the farm, get gas," she said. "Honestly, anything I could think of to stay occupied."

No mention of John's Auto Shop, Carla noted.

She decided she just needed to rip the Band-aid off and go for it.

"Nessie, I need to ask you something and I don't want you to get mad at me," she said.

A look of confusion and concern swept over Vanessa's face as she turned toward her sister. Carla took a deep breath and spun out the lie she had created to get to the truth.

"I was cleaning yesterday, and I put some clean clothes in your room," she said, shifting in her seat. "And I made your bed for you."

Carla paused to see if her sister would react, but her sister just seemed more confused.

"There was something sticking out from under the mattress," she continued. "I couldn't help but check to see what it was."

Vanessa took another sip from her tea, seemingly unvexed by the story.

"Nessie, it was a knife," Carla finally said.

The words landed between them like a heavy accusation. Vanessa smiled sadly.

"Norm put that there," she said softly. "He said I needed some kind of self-defense when he was off on fishing trips. He wanted to give me a gun, but I refused. I had completely forgotten that knife was there."

Her words were soft and melancholy, not nervous at all. Normally, Carla would believe her. But now she didn't know what to believe anymore. But that was just one of her questions.

"There's something else I was wondering about," Carla said. "When you went to the beach last night, you were gone a really long time."

Vanessa nodded. "I've been thinking about that."

She sat her mug of tea down.

"I think I somehow knew," she said. "I mean, I was sound asleep and then I woke up feeling overwhelmed with sadness and feelings I didn't understand. I had to get some air. And then, for some weird reason, I felt this urge to go to the beach.

"You know, that's the beach where Norm and I went on our first date," she continued. "It's where we went to celebrate getting this house. It was our place, I guess. And I sat there, watching the waves, and suddenly felt so, so sad. So empty. For no reason. I can't explain it."

She leaned forward and grabbed her sister's hands.

"And I know this sounds stupid, but then I felt this lightness. Just out of the blue. It was just for a few seconds, but it literally took my breath away."

Vanessa's eyes had welled up with tears.

"I think it was Norm," she said. "I mean, that's around the time when he must have...I think he was saying goodbye."

She smiled weakly, then crumbled under her sadness. Carla put her tea down and pulled her grieving sister to her as she sobbed uncontrollably into her shoulder. Carla felt horrible for Vanessa and also incredibly guilty for ever even entertaining the thought that she could be a killer.

Carla held her sister and comforted her for over a half hour, never saying a word. Just letting her grieve. Letting her know she was there for her. Vanessa's sobs slowly lightened, and she finally pulled away, wiping away all the tears. She was just about to say something when they were both startled by a loud knock at the door.

51

DETECTIVE TURNER TAPPED ON THE PASSENGER WINDOW OF
Norm's work truck. Sam had parked it down the road from
John's Auto Shop in the same spot where Carla had parked
earlier. He nodded at Turner as he opened the passenger door.
The detective climbed inside, immediately flinching at the fish
smell.

"Holy shit," Turner said. "At least roll the windows down,
man."

"You get used to it after a while," Sam said, complying to
Turner's request and rolling down the windows.

"You know, that's not a good thing," Turner said. "So what is
this all about?"

"Thanks for coming," Sam said.

"Yeah, well, I only did it because I felt guilty about my chief
calling your boss," Turner said. "I didn't mean for him to do
that."

Sam shrugged it off.

"No big deal," he said. "I had it coming."

He pointed up toward John's shop and was about to tell his
theory, but Turner interrupted.

"No, it is a big deal," he said. "I've been thinking and I owe you an apology."

"Great. Fine. Apology accepted," Sam said impatiently.

"You've been trying to help and I've been an asshole," Turner said.

"I overstepped my bounds," Sam said, wanting to get to the task at hand. "But it was nothing personal. Just a bad habit of mine. Anyway..."

"I'm sorry if it got you in trouble," Turner said.

Sam sighed, giving into Turner's need to hash this out right now.

"I'm always in trouble with that asshole," Sam said. "And after the whole thing with Norm, I definitely had it coming."

"True," Turner said. "But you've been trying to help and I've been treating you like an annoyance instead of an ally. This is a big case, and it's got me a little stressed out."

"Speaking of the case," Sam said, steering the conversation back to why he had asked Turner to meet him.

"I'm saying that I could use your help," Turner said, impatient with Sam's seeming denseness.

"That's great and we'll all sing Kumbaya around a campfire later," Sam said. "But right now I need you to listen."

Sam told Turner about how Carla accidentally caught John and Gina together at his auto shop.

"Gina?" Turner said, clearly surprised. "The nurse?"

Sam nodded and shared his theory about John wanting to get rid of Jane, especially with her now being pregnant.

"Jane was pregnant?" Turner yelled. "Hang on. How do you know this and I don't?"

"Gina told Carla," Sam said. "I figured you knew by now from the autopsy."

Turner shook his head, clearly angry.

"I haven't heard jack shit from those assholes," he said.

He pushed his anger down and concentrated on Sam's theory, finally shaking his head.

"I've known John my entire life," he said. "I know his faults—and he's got a lot of them, to be sure. But he's not a murderer. I know this for a fact."

Sam started to protest, but Turner interrupted him.

"John was at my house on the night Norm was murdered," he said. "He had come over earlier and had had a lot to drink. Pretty upset about the whole Jane thing."

Not too upset to start banging her best friend, Sam thought.

"I didn't want him driving drunk, so I let him sleep it off," Turner continued. "When I got the call about the murder, he was still sleeping in the guest room. He'd been there all night."

Sam was shocked. Talk about your perfect alibi.

"Still, I would like to talk to him," Turner said, stepping out of the truck. "This whole thing with Gina raises some flags for sure."

As he walked toward the auto shop, he turned and looked back at a stunned Sam.

"You coming or not?" Turner asked.

The two men walked up the hill to the auto shop. Sam's mind was spinning as he tried to find any shrapnel left after Turner had blown up his theory. When they reached the office door, Turner knocked. When there was no answer, he tried to open it, but the door was locked. The two men walked to the garage entrance as well, but, even though it was the middle of the day, everything seemed locked up.

"Where the hell is he?" Turner asked.

"Hey, Turner," Sam said. "How much do you know about Gina Moffet?"

52

As Vanessa scurried to her bedroom to clean up her tear-stained face, Carla got up to answer the knock. When she opened the door, her stomach did a flip.

It was John Rowe.

He seemed as confused to see Carla standing there as she did to see him.

"Is, uh, Vanessa here?" he stammered.

"She's busy," Carla answered, blocking the doorway so it was clear she had no intention of letting John in.

Suddenly, a realization hit John, and he smiled.

"You're the sister," he said. "I'm John..."

"I know who you are," Carla interrupted. "Like I said, my sister's busy."

"If you wouldn't mind telling her I'm here," he said gently. "She's expecting me."

Expecting him? Carla thought. *Not likely.*

"John?" Vanessa said from behind Carla.

Carla turned as Vanessa walked toward them. Even though she had tried to clean up, her eyes were still puffy. She smiled at John and waved for him to come inside.

"Come in," she said.

A confused Carla stepped to the side, glaring at John as he walked past her. John smiled weakly and offered a slight nod, as if to reassure her he meant no harm. Carla couldn't help but notice the sadness in his eyes. Not that he was mourning Jane's death. He clearly seemed to have moved on with that. It was the permanent sadness of a person who had lost in life too many times.

"I'm sorry to barge in," he said. "I forgot your sister was here."

He extended his hand to Carla.

"I'm John."

Carla shook his hand and introduced herself.

"Do you want some tea?" Vanessa asked. "A beer?"

John shook his head.

"I can't stay long. I just wanted to..."

He glanced at Carla, not sure if he should finish the sentence.

What was going on? Carla wondered.

Vanessa nodded nervously.

"Carla, do you mind?" Vanessa asked.

"Car stuff," John offered unconvincingly.

"Very private car stuff, apparently," Carla replied.

"It's about Norm," Vanessa said.

Something about Norm that Vanessa didn't want to share?

"I'll be in the back," Carla stammered, pointing toward the bedrooms.

She turned and walked into Vanessa's bedroom, leaving her sister alone with the man who could be linked to the murder of her husband.

What are they talking about?

Carla strained to listen through the door, ready to pounce if things got out of hand. But all she could make out were muffled whispers. Suddenly, Carla jumped in surprise at a loud banging at the front door.

53

JOHN WATCHED AS VANESSA WENT DOWN THE HALL TO ANSWER the door and was confused when he saw who followed her back in.

It was Gina.

She was wearing nurse scrubs that were covered in smiley face emojis and was clutching a handbag that was hanging off of one shoulder. But there was something about her that was off.

"Hi, John," Gina said, barely acknowledging Vanessa's presence.

Her presence clearly startled him.

"I tried to call you, but you weren't answering," she explained, noting his nervous confusion. "My necklace was missing, so I figured I left it at your shop. I was on my way there but then I saw you coming this way so I followed."

She walked past Vanessa, focused completely on John.

"I don't have your necklace," John said nervously.

"It's probably at the shop," Gina said, turning to look at Vanessa for the first time. "I hope I wasn't interrupting anything."

Vanessa shook her head, noticing a spark of menace behind the nurse's sweet smile.

"I just needed to drop something off," John explained.

"That's okay, honey," she said.

Vanessa was stunned as she figured out the relationship between Gina and John.

"You two are a..."

"Oh, he didn't tell you?" Gina asked.

She turned to John.

"You're not doing anything you shouldn't be doing, are you?" she said with a wink.

The fire in her eyes was growing and John was clearly nervous.

"Of course not!" he said.

"You think that me and John...?" Vanessa asked. "I swear. There's nothing going on between us."

Gina spun around and glared at Vanessa.

"Because he's with me now," Gina snapped. "Just me."

Vanessa gasped, taking a step back from the sudden outburst. Gina too a breath to collect herself. The glare in her eyes disappeared and her sweet smile came back.

"I just know how irresistible he is," she continued. "But he's mine."

Vanessa nodded. Even though Gina seemed to have calmed down, something about her still seemed off.

"I think you need to leave," Vanessa said firmly.

"I think you need to stay away from my man," Gina shot back.

"Okay, everyone calm down," John said, extending his arms to Gina. "Baby, there's nothing going on here."

"You know, I saw the two of you," Gina said, the menace returning to her eyes. "Back at the shop. All friendly and cuddly. It broke my heart."

Both John and Vanessa were caught speechless.

"Thought you were being so secretive, didn't you?" Gina said.

"You've got it all wrong," John offered.

"That's what you like, right John?" Gina asked. "Keeping everything a secret?"

She shook her head as the anger continued to rage inside her.

"I haven't gone through all of this just to be tossed aside," she said through gritted teeth.

"Gina, nothing is going on here," Vanessa said.

Gina shot a glare at Vanessa that nearly knocked her down.

"Couldn't keep your greedy hands off of him, could you?" Gina sneered. "I guess once a whore, always a whore."

"Gina!" Carla yelled, getting everyone's attention.

Carla appeared out of the hallway and walked next to her sister.

"What the hell is going on?" she asked.

Caught up in her anger, Gina glared at Carla.

"So you know about the two of them?" Gina asked.

"Know what?" Carla asked back.

A look of contempt fell over Gina's face.

"You've known about them all along, haven't you?" Gina accused. "Even when I told you about Jane. You knew about them then and said nothing."

"Know what?" Carla asked. "I don't know what you're talking about."

"Enough lies!" Gina yelled.

Tears began to stream down her face and she started to tremble as she turned to John.

"I've done everything for you," she said softly. "And this is how you thank me?"

"Why don't we go outside and talk?" John suggested, trying to sound calm and reassuring.

But Gina shook her head.

"No. It's too late for that now."

The sadness boiled into fury as Gina reached into her handbag and pulled out a gun.

54

TURNER SAT IN HIS CAR WAITING FOR THE DISPATCHER TO GET back to him. Sam had left, having been assured by Turner that Gina not only had been nothing but a model citizen since she'd been on the island, but they had done a background check on her and there was no criminal history.

Still, he couldn't get the notion out of his head. What did he really know about her? And how long had she and John been sleeping together? He needed to talk to John. As certain as he was about his friend's innocence, he had to admit it definitely didn't look good.

He had decided to pay Gina a visit. At least talk to her about everything. Get her take. Then he had a second idea. The background check had been based on Gina's name. But what about the fingerprint database? He knew all hospital employees had fingerprints on file, so he had called his dispatcher and asked to have a search pulled on Gina's fingerprints.

"Turner? You there?" the female dispatcher's voice came through over the police radio.

Turner snapped up the mic. "Whaddaya got?"

"I've got a lot," the dispatcher said. "First off, our girl Gina is an alias. Her actual name is Tina McMillan. From Denver. And she's got quite the rap sheet. Assault. Harassment. Stalking. Arson. And attempted murder."

"Come again?" Turner asked, shocked at what he had just heard.

"I'm digging deeper on the attempted murder," the dispatcher said. "But from what I can tell, the victim was stabbed multiple times and somehow lived. Charges were dropped, but I don't know why."

Probably not enough evidence to prosecute, thought Turner.

"I need you to issue an APB out on Gina Moffet," Turner said. "We need to contact all the departments on the island. We're going to have to divide and conquer on this and track her down as soon as possible."

As Turner spoke, he started his car and pulled out on to the road in front of the auto shop. He reached into his jacket pocket to get the business card Sam had just given to him, dialing the number into his phone. The phone rang as Turner sped down the road. But Sam didn't answer.

55

Sam pulled up to Vanessa's house, wondering about the two strange cars in the driveway. As he got closer, he noticed one car had a hospital parking sticker on the corner of the rear window.

It must be Gina, he thought. *But why would she be here? And who does the other car belong to?*

He got out of the truck and walked toward the house, leaving his phone on the passenger seat. By the time he reached the front door, he was too far away to hear it ringing.

He stepped inside and walked unwittingly into the living area. Stunned, he froze in place, trying to make sense of what he was seeing.

There was a crazed woman wearing smiley face nurse's scrubs standing in the middle of the living room, waving a gun back and forth between Vanessa, Carla and John Rowe.

"Don't come any closer!" Gina yelled.

"I knew it!" Sam shouted out without thinking.

He was so pleased with himself for being right in suspecting Gina that he temporarily forgot the gravity of the predicament.

"I said, don't come closer," Gina yelled again.

Sam stopped, still grinning.

"Paul is gonna be so pissed when he finds out," Sam said.

"Shut up and stay still," Gina said.

Sam nodded.

"I'm assuming you're Gina," he said. "I'm going to be so let down if you're not."

"Be quiet," she snapped at him.

Sam nodded, taking that as a yes. As he began to come down from the high of being right, he glanced around to gauge the situation. He was too far away from Gina to run at her. She'd at least get one shot out before he could disarm her. His only option was to talk the gun out of her hand, and hostage negotiation had never been his strong suit.

The gun. He recognized that gun.

"I'm Sam, by the way," he said casually.

"I know who you are," Gina shot back.

"I didn't know if you recognized me," Sam said, slowly taking another step forward "Last time you saw me, it was from behind."

She glared at Sam, waving the gun to motion for him to stop. But he took another step anyway.

"That really hurt, by the way," Sam said, rubbing the back of his head. "And it was totally uncalled for."

Gina seemed surprised that Sam had figured out she had been his attacker.

"I see you still have my gun," Sam said, pointing to the pistol that was pointed at him. "Thank God you didn't get rid of it. Do you know they were gonna take it out of my paycheck?"

"Wait," Carla said, making the connection that Gina must have been Sam's attacker.

"I should have killed you, too," Gina snarled.

"But you didn't," Sam said, taking yet another step.

"Because you're not all bad, are you, Gina? In fact, I'd bet you didn't even want to kill Norm."

Vanessa gasped out loud at the accusation. John's face froze in shock and disbelief.

"I gave him every chance," Gina explained. "All he had to do was leave town. But he wouldn't."

She waved her gun at Vanessa.

"I told him I'd kill you if he ever showed his face again," she said. "But he wouldn't leave. He said he had to see you one last time. I knew right then what I had to do. It was the only way to be sure he'd stay quiet."

"You...killed..." Vanessa could barely get the words out.

Gina looked at her and shrugged. "Sorry. It was him or me."

While Gina was focused on Vanessa, Sam took another step forward. He was now only about ten feet away.

Gina spun the gun back around to Sam.

"Would you stay still?" she yelled.

"I'm sorry!" Sam yelled back. "Having a gun pointed at my face makes me restless!"

The outburst stunned Gina, just as Sam had hoped it would.

"I guess it is kind of romantic," Sam said. "Killing for love. I get it."

"Don't," Gina warned.

"That must have sucked, though," Sam continued. "You and John fall in love. You finally meet the man of your dreams. But he's still stuck in a relationship with another woman."

Carla took a step to the side and Vanessa caught the reflection of the knife Carla was still clutching behind her back.

"But then the real kicker," Sam said. "She had to go and get pregnant."

"Shut up!" Gina yelled.

"Wait. What?" John muttered, completely stunned. "Jane was pregnant?"

"Oops," Sam said. "You didn't know? Ouch."

John glared at Gina. "Is all this true?"

Gina looked at John, suddenly softening.

"I couldn't let her trap you, Baby," Gina said. "We were meant to be together."

Rage was building in John. "You bitch," he yelled as he stormed toward her.

Gina fired the gun, and the noise echoed through the house. John yelled out in anguish as he grabbed his leg and fell to the floor.

The shot threw everyone off and before Carla even realized what was happening, Vanessa had pulled the knife away from her and ran toward Gina.

Gina spun around, the pistol aimed directly at Vanessa's head, but Vanessa reached her before she could fire, slashing her forearm as they both toppled to the ground.

Gina yelled in pain and dropped the gun. Sam took advantage of the commotion, lunging across the room and pinning Gina to the floor.

"No!" Gina yelled manically.

Sam straddled Gina's stomach as she flailed underneath him like a trapped wild animal. Carla grabbed the gun and handed it to Sam.

"Hello, old friend," Sam said to his pistol. "Did the mean lady treat you nice?"

"Let me go!" Gina yelled.

"Sorry, Nurse Ratched," Sam yelled. "But I'm already on the shit list of the local police. I think they'd frown upon that."

"Let her go," came a disturbingly calm voice behind Sam.

He turned to see Vanessa still clutching the knife in her hands, pointing it at Sam.

56

"Vanessa, what are you doing?" Carla asked.

"Let me finish what I started," Vanessa said.

Her body was shaking, but she had a fierce determination in her eyes.

"She killed my husband," Vanessa yelled.

"Vanessa, you don't want to do this," Carla said gently.

"She's right," John said.

Vanessa looked over at John, confused. He was lying in the ground, holding his bloodied leg where Gina had shot him.

"She killed Jane," Vanessa argued. "She killed your..."

"I know what she did," John interrupted before she could say more. "But don't let her take everything. She deserves to spend the rest of her life in prison. Not you."

"And trust me," Sam said. "Prison is not gonna be any fun for someone like her."

Carla stepped next to Vanessa and gently put her hand over the hand holding the knife. Vanessa slowly released her grip and collapsed in sobs.

"If you want, you can punch her in the face before the cops get here," Sam offered.

Carla looked at him, shaking her head in disapproval. Sam shrugged.

Carla rushed over to John to tend to his wound.

Vanessa called 9-1-1 and Gina, finally surrendering to her fate, stopped struggling.

"Damn, Nessie," Sam said. "You went all Samurai on us there."

It managed to get a smile out of Vanessa and the four sat in silence as they waited for the police to arrive.

57

SAM LOOKED OUT THE WINDOW, LETTING OUT A PRIVATE SIGH OF relief as the plane's wheels touched the ground. For some reason, he felt safe, even though he was still strapped in a large metal tube that was traveling at dangerous speeds while balancing on three small wheels.

"Home sweet home," he said to himself.

Carla squeezed his arm lovingly in agreement.

They had stayed in Martha's Vineyard for another week, helping close out the case and be there for Vanessa at Norm's funeral. Even though the conditions were morbid, Sam had actually found some time to enjoy himself. Not one to deal directly with grief, Jude seized the opportunity to distract himself by serving as an unofficial tour guide for Sam. He not only took him to the favorite tourist sites, like Jaws Bridge and the Gingerbread Houses of Oak Bluffs, but also some local favorites, like the hiking trails in the Great Rock Bight Preserve and the colorful cliffs at Aquinnah. He even took Sam and Turner out deep-sea fishing.

But Sam was ready to return to work, mainly because he couldn't wait to rub the fact that he had helped solve a double murder into Chief Bannon's face. Turner had even made a point of calling Chief Bannon personally to applaud Sam's invaluable help. A favor that Sam admittedly had to "buy" with a couple rounds of beer at The Dive In.

Carla had invited her sister to come visit her in Texas. Vanessa had promised to take the trip as soon as she sorted everything out and saw the lavender farm through the busy tourist season. Knowing she had Jude there helped ease Carla's concerns.

It turned out the reason Vanessa had visited John was to borrow money to help cover Norm's funeral costs until she received his life insurance. At first, Carla was angry that Vanessa hadn't come to her for help, but her sister explained that she had swallowed so much pride during Carla's visit, she couldn't bring herself to ask for yet another favor.

Gina pled guilty to the murders of Jane Caplan and Norm Mayhew. In lieu of her guilty plea, which would most certainly result in life imprisonment, the state chose not to seek a more challenging third murder charge for Jane's unborn child.

According to Gina's official statement, she had arrived at Jane's house around 1:00 a.m. and stabbed her fifteen times in the chest, throat and torso. She then wiped down the house for fingerprints and other signs of evidence and was about to leave when Norm walked in on the crime scene.

After watching Norm stumble through the crime scene drunk, leaving fingerprints everywhere he went, Gina realized she had a perfect scapegoat. She lied to Norm, telling him she didn't act alone and her partner would murder Vanessa if anything happened to her. She told him the only way to save his wife would be to disappear forever. Too drunk to question her threat, Norm panicked and agreed.

As soon as she heard the detective from Texas was looking for Norm, Gina started following him. When she saw him take a late-night ferry to Cape Cod with Jude, she got on the same ferry and trailed them to Norm's mobile home. She was sneaking up on the house when she heard the rifle blast and saw Jude jump out of his truck. Hidden in the shadows, she was able to sneak up behind him and clock him in the back of the skull with a rock. Maybe it was because of his age, or maybe she got lucky and hit a sweet spot, but he instantly dropped to the ground, knocked out cold.

She then snuck into the trailer home, rock still in hand, and hit Sam on the back of the head. She had quickly grabbed his pistol and argued with Norm before shooting him in cold blood. She was currently being held at MCI-Cedar Junction, a maximum-security penitentiary southwest of Boston, awaiting a full psychiatric evaluation before her official sentencing.

Carla slid her fingers in Sam's, bringing him back to reality. He turned to find her looking up at him and smiling.

"You're cute when you're thinking," she teased. "You should do that more often."

Sam grinned back. "It would lose its luster if I did it all the time, Baby," he said. "Gotta keep things fresh. Don't want you to get bored."

Carla kissed Sam gently on the lips.

"I think it's pretty safe to say I'm never going to get bored with you in my life, Sam Lawson."

He laughed. "For the record," he said. "You pulled me into this little adventure."

"You know how it is," she said with a wink. "Got to keep things fresh."

THE END

Thank you for reading
DARK HARBOR
If you enjoyed it, please be sure to leave a review wherever you
bought your copy.

GET A FREE COPY OF *BOUND BY MURDER*
Go back to Sam Lawson's first murder case in this fun and
riveting e-novella. To get your free copy, visit
davidkwilsonauthor.com

MORE SAM LAWSON MYSTERIES:

COMBUSTIBLE

BENEATH THE SURFACE

DEADLY REPUTATION

ALSO BY DAVID K. WILSON:

RED DIRT BLUES
"Wildly entertaining and absurdly funny!" Nothing goes as
planned when a cold-blooded thief is pulled into the quirky
and colorful lives of a motley crew of rednecks.

Learn more at davidkwilsonauthor.com

ACKNOWLEDGMENTS

It truly takes a village to write a book and there are so many people to thank, I can't possibly list them all. But here are a few...

Thanks to Ashley Previte, who introduced me to Martha's Vineyard and helped me bring it to life in this book. And a big thanks to Shelley Upchurch, whose insights and input were invaluable (that's a lot of in's). I also want to thank Arte Levy and Wesley Hicks for their technical advice, Caroline Johnson for her fantastic cover design and Cyndi Stripling for her keen proofreading eye. And I am filled with gratitude for the help, advice and support of a special group of readers and fellow writers, including Lorraine Evanoff, Yvonne Pelletier and James Hewitson.

Finally, special thanks also goes out to Colin Wilson and Mallory Wilson for their input and opinions. And just for putting up with me in general.

And thank YOU for reading *Dark Harbor*! I hope you enjoyed it.

ABOUT THE AUTHOR

David K. Wilson grew up in East Texas, surrounded by enough colorful characters to fill the pages of hundreds of books. He has been an advertising copywriter and creative director, and is probably responsible for some of the junk mail you've received. He is also a seasoned ghostwriter and screenwriter. He currently lives in upstate New York, where he still complains about winter every single year.

Sign up to receive updates on David's next novel at
davidkwilsonauthor.com.

f facebook.com/davidkwilsonauthor
instagram.com/davidkwilsonauthor
g goodreads.com/davidkwilson

Made in the USA
Coppell, TX
04 April 2022

75986172R00132